ISBN: 978-0-9559883-0-1

Front cover photograph by: Wit
Rear cover photograph by: Rachel Scott

Acknowledgements

I would like to thank the following:
Laura Douglas for her valuable help, Alice – Mary for reading and
persisting with the drafts, Pat O'Connor MBE for her support,
CJW the IT wizard and extra special thanks to my sister Evelyn,
my niece Leah Williams and to the two women who were the inspiration
of the novel - LaToya Aisha and Serena Clare – may we soon be together.

CONSEQUENCES?

Harry James

Prologue:

Sally Geyer took a bite of the wholemeal cheese sandwich she had prepared that morning and walked to the window of the classroom. The sight of the busy playground was a testament that too few of the children went home to lunch – those that did were envied, but branded spoilt.

People had funny ideas about the country, Sally mused. Her friends from college who had stayed in London and taught inner-city kids often talked as though she spent idyllic days in a West Country blur, ringed around with rosy-cheeked mini-yokels who walked to school across the red and green fields, humming songs about Grey Mares and Uncle Tom Cobley.

What they needed was a couple of weeks with the hard-bitten tykes from Mutley Plain who bussed in from the suburbs of Plymouth. Half of them with granddads laid off from the shipyard and fathers who hardly expected to find work at all. Needed them though, or the school which served a small village and the farms around, would be under threat from its falling rolls.

The playground had been understaffed at break and the sudden increase in the noise level that came faintly through the window shutting out a raw November day grabbed Sally's attention.

As her eyes scoured the playground, she could see that a group of around seven children had formed a circle. Instincts honed from years as a primary school teacher informed her that something extra troublesome was going on. Where were the precious midday supervisors when you needed them? Furthermore, who cared if Zoe Coombes had sodding time-of-the-month problems (twice a month, seemingly)? If she couldn't do playground duty she should say so while there was time to change the rota.

On opening the window, Sally immediately caught the loud taunting voices of the children who were singing "Brown girl in the ring". Sally took a chestful of air, but before she had time to shout out, a slim white woman in her late twenties marched purposefully through the ring of intimidating children.

Even from this distance, the horrified teacher felt the woman's rage. Her shoulders lifted and quivering, her stride was close to a rush as she shouted out words that could not be heard; yet Sally knew were aggressive. Sally's concern shifted; it was the tormentors who were at risk now, and whether it served them right or not, she couldn't have mothers laying into them. Sally's shout turned heads.

Now that the little girl had been pulled clear and clamped close under her mother's arm, Sally recognised Andrea easily. She was the only mixed race child at Styne Oak Junior School. There were the Chinese restaurant children and Ahmed the newsagent's youngest son, but somehow Andrea was always on her own.

For the first time Sally saw how alike the two were. Good-looking both of them, tall, long legs and necks, fine-boned, a challenging set to their heads, though where the woman's dark blonde hair was clipped up in a swirl that waved down her back, the child had a cloud of close natural curls. Even fear could not make Andrea appear anything less dignified than bewildered.

There had never been anything like this before. What were they going to do about it thought Sally who was now bracing herself for the walk to the Head's door? And anyway, she was too late. Andrea's small pointed face turned for a moment as her mother swept her away, in response to Sally's call. That was all the comfort she had.

Chapter 1

Marcus Carpenter raised his shaven head from under the duvet, stretched out his arms lethargically before swinging his legs out of the double bed. He brought his six-foot, well-built frame upright and dressed only in boxer shorts, walked to the television set, switched it on before making himself a cup of black coffee. The caffeine was necessary to face the day, any day, that all seemed the same now.

Even though the bed-sit was modest and somewhat sparsely furnished, with only a few nondescript posters adorning the wall, Marcus had managed to keep it fairly clean.

He had acquired a decent music system, which might have been the main focus of the room, not the bed or the sofa that nestled beside the warm friendly radiator. Instead, it was the large domineering colour television with video, which was the real focus of the bed-sit that had been equipped almost entirely on a single trip to Ikea in Croydon.

He had been 'ill' back then and Ayesha, his social worker, had taken him there in her roomy old estate.

With Ayesha's help, he could have achieved a bright, homely look; perhaps fitted his little abode with cheerful colours and smart little space-saving fitments. A cheery, spotted breakfast and dinner set for one ... co-ordinating quilt and pillows; sunflower-splashed voile curtains called 'Primpta' had been all within his means. The final effect could have been similar to a room in a modestly priced bed and breakfast, or a cheap hotel. However, Marcus hadn't been up to it.

As things stood, the curtains were pale mushroom, the crockery white, the ready-framed prints were abstract in shades of olive and brown. The bed-sit was not particularly warm or inviting (in fact Marcus still didn't consider it home - accommodation was the right word), which was underlined by the lack of any ornaments, photographs or trace of connections. It definitely had the look and feel of a reclusive single man.

He went back to the bed where he lay propped like an invalid, remote in hand watching the morning chat show. For a full hour, he watched vigilantly, as if his life depended upon it.

Throughout the proceedings – the distresses and the tears, the comforting and the confrontations of the walking wounded who had come to share their most intimate wounds; secrets now made public to the millions of faceless unknown viewers, Marcus' face remained calm and unmoved. From time to time, he nodded and made an "mmmh-hmmm" deep in his mouth, like the swallowed shadow of an acknowledgment.

When the programme ended, Marcus checked the clock beside the bed, rose up lazily and walked to the bathroom. This room was the one redeeming feature, the piece-de-resistance. Equipped with a modern walk-in power shower, tasteful cream fittings, it was as if all the real imaginative efforts and thought had been put into this room.

He rubbed his eyes, flushed the loo then walked back to the main living area and looked out of the window that gave a splendid view onto a mixed street of offices, convenience retail stores and flats. It was quite a good street with apartments moving up the scale, subject to endless refurbishments from property developers who had homed in on affordable blocks whose postcode inner-city-centre location gave promises of stratospheric rents.

He noticed the familiar shape of a young white woman burdened with luggage walking towards him, her straight brown hair catching the sunlight, sending out rainbow sparks of bronze and gold. She was dressed in denim jeans and jacket, humping a holdall that bounced awkwardly against her fragile leg (which might even have been bruising it). Her body bent ungainly under the weight of the rucksack she had stuffed with books. His eyes followed her as she made her way trickily down the street and turned at last into his block.

When she disappeared from his view, Marcus snapped back to the now, went to the 'kitchen' area of the bed-sit and opened the fridge. After a cursory glance which confirmed that no fresh fruit, no green stuff was within; he removed the two remaining eggs and half a tin of baked beans then delved a second time for a plastic carton and proceeded to make himself a micro-waved omelette of sorts.

He beat the eggs in a bowl, added a splash of boiling water and a sliver of the horrible pearlized spread from the carton. It was a joyless meal for a man who had been used to taking care of himself, who had previously used freshly chopped herbs in an herb-

4

chopping gadget from Habitat and sang the praises of a pestle and mortar for pounding spices.

Neither was it a meal for a man who had regularly dined in restaurants. They might not have been expensive eateries, but Maxine had always known how to find the good ones.

Both he and Maxine had disliked mass-produced, processed food, preferring to patronize small, local shops; ones with tempting trays and boxes out on the pavement, shops that had baskets brimming with fruit and vegetables imported from all the warm corners of the earth, smelling of earth and rind when it was sunny in London.

Towards the end of their marriage – when he was earning really well – Maxine would take the car and make trips to Waitrose in Chingford. It wasn't purely for the 'Fairtrade' policies of the supermarket's buyers that Maxine favoured this brand.

Marcus always had doubted deep down, how much she really cared about saving the whale, and protecting dolphins, or paying Third World farmers a proper price for their coffee beans. She wasn't a bleeding heart type, but she liked the taste of its classy products, and knew from her women friends that they had snob value, as well as the moral high ground. Even at their son's playgroup, all the top mothers shopped at Waitrose. Maxine had been an aspirational wife with a healthy appetite.

Now when he shopped for himself, he had to be selective. Neglecting the years of practice, which had taught him that cheap did not always represent value - 'needs must' - now meant that compromise was the sad fact.

Meanwhile, Natasha pushed open the door to Lambton House by turning her back and leaning against it. After this manoeuvre, she dropped her holdall for respite and slipped her fingers under the rucksack straps to ease the pressure. The reddening of that too thin skin where the nylon webbing had chafed would last for days. After a necessary rest, she took up her gear again and prepared to trudge up the two flights of stairs that lead to her father's flat. There was no happy lift of her chin or to the corners of her full, sweet mouth as she climbed.

She fished for her key, took a deep breath before she inserted it into the lock and tentatively eased the door slightly ajar. Thankfully,

5

the flat was quiet. Natasha hurriedly carried her luggage through to a small bedroom and closed the door behind her.

Marcus placed the plate, mug and bowl in the small sink before ambling back to the window. His eyes widened fractionally as he steadily became more alert. Another young woman; polished and presented this time, wearing a smart white trouser suit that sang a duet with her cafè-au-lait skin tones, opened the door of a gold BMW that was parked opposite his block. He drank in her long shapely legs and ample bosom as she slid stylishly behind the wheel before gunning the engine and driving away.

Marcus' mouth hardened at the woman's competent performance of being drop-dead gorgeous. As his life had shrunk, so had the play of his facial expressions; his feelings now displayed in small contractions of the muscles as if he were economizing and could not afford anything more expansive. It had been a long time since he had experienced such emotions.

When the night drew in and tiredness took over, Marcus switched off the TV and cried himself to sleep.

Chapter 2

Another new day at Lambton House. No weather to notice, not fair or foul. Nothing weather. But, having got through the 'non-day' before, Marcus was up and about a lot earlier. He checked the clock again; it was 9.30 a.m. In fact, the wry thought came to Marcus, yesterday had not been quite the 'nothing-day' of his routine of late. There had been the two women to mull over. Natasha the student girl who couldn't manage her baggage – probably still sleeping, and the fancy mixed-race bitch across the road. Jellicoe Street was becoming almost eventful for those who took small part in the business of living.

Agitatedly, the man who had once been a long-limbed athlete shifted around on the edge of his bed, flicking the TV from channel to channel until he heard the sound he had been waiting for. At last. At last.

Marcus reached blindly for his puffa jacket, darted to the front door, and swooped like a gannet to pick up his mail; a solitary, familiar brown envelope that he knew contained a girocheque.

As he closed the front door and checked that it was firmly locked, Natasha emerged from her father's flat at the top of the stairs. The lack of the heavy rucksack had improved her posture and she now looked all of her five foot, six inches.

"Hi Marcus," Natasha said with her first, fleeting smile in hours.

"Oh hello," answered Marcus who had become unaccustomed to having a conversation. He scratched his flaky skinned face, "Back for your holidays?" he added tamely.

"Yes."

As he put the keys into his pocket, Marcus felt the giro. The need to cash it became paramount. "Good, I'm sorry but I've got to rush. I'll see you around though. Bye," and was off without thinking whether Natasha was going his way.

"I guess so. Bye," Natasha said quietly as she in turn made her way out of Lambton House.

Marcus hurried to join the queue for the Post Office, trying not to look at the numerous young mothers pushing buggies with children of varying ages, the pensioners, the so called 'no-hopers' and idlers as he waited anxiously to change the giro into *real* money.

Once the cashier had given him his cash, Marcus bought a weekly bus pass and caught a bus to Lewisham.

Throughout the ten-minute journey, he stared absently out of the window watching the background change from grandiose Victorian properties with their well maintained gardens, to the congested modern mass produced houses of the varying estates that had grown ever larger. Abandoned cars and litter strewn pavements clearly signposted the demarcation lines.

Marcus stopped off at the library, spending an hour surfing the internet on the free access computers the Council had provided. As usual, he had no e-mails. When his hour was up, he made his way to the fiction section and selected three books that might provide relief and distraction from his endless diet of daytime TV.

He emerged into the spring sunshine and made his way to the market, a fortnightly highlight he could still enjoy. In addition, if he left it until late morning, the stall owners were beginning to give bargain weight. Local byelaws insisted the market be gone by two p.m., so by noon the vendors would be shouting the odds.

The cries of "Pound a bowl, pound a bowl," rang out from all directions as Marcus navigated his way through the crowded streets, tolerating the hustle bustle and increasingly unfamiliar contact with strangers. Market stalls that once been manned by local traders who could tell stories of the Blitz and beyond had passed onto Asian, Kosovan and Eastern Europeans who had migrated to London in search of a better future.

Fuck political correctness, Marcus thought and made a conscious decision to give his custom (regardless how measly) to one of the increasingly rare local traders. His ears pricked up like antennae when he heard the familiar "loverly termaters" shout of the white greengrocer.

Now that he was a man living alone in a bed-sit, he had lost the luxury of buying big quantities, even at knockdown prices. Nevertheless, Marcus haggled quite happily for salad stuff, a fine avocado, along with a hand of bananas and two apples. It was enough to make him feel almost a member of the human race again.

As he strode back towards the bus stop, he noticed the increasing number of shops that were now advertising the fact that they sold Polish goods. Yet another sign of the transformation that was taking place in London.

Prior to boarding a bus back to Blackheath, he stopped in the conveniently handy Lidl and diligently went about selecting the depressing cheap staples that his budget allowed. Purchases complete he joined the queue of mainly Eastern Europeans, ignoring the contemptuous stares they felt his black skin merited and paid for his goods before making his way to his local pub.

The *Market Tavern* was fairly busy with its usual diverse mix of clientele that ranged from the local regulars - drinkers who hadn't the time or the inflated salaries for wine bars further afield - to the suited workers of the many offices that lay within walking distance of the popular pub.

Marcus sat alone in a quiet corner drinking a pint of lager, the three supermarket carrier bags that contained his carefully selected supplies sitting safely at his feet under the table, when a smartly dressed ginger-haired man of around twenty-eight entered the pub. He looked around the other tables before he noticed Marcus and waved.

He walked to the bar, removing his tie as he ordered two pints, then joined Marcus and handed him one of the glasses.

Marcus nodded his head in appreciation. "Cheers Declan."

"No problem mate. How are things?" Declan said in a mild Irish brogue as he took off his coat and threw it on the empty chair.

"Still alive," Marcus answered sullenly.

Declan took his pint, clinked his glass with Marcus' before taking a long swig. "That was needed," he smiled. "Might have some good news for you mate."

"What's that?"

"I was speaking to a client today; he mentioned he was looking for new staff."

"Yeah?" Marcus said with little interest.

"Come on Marcus. I'm trying to help you out here."

"Sorry mate. It's just that I've sent out so many letters, application forms and answered so many adverts. What's the fucking point?"

"I know its hard mate, but you've got to keep on trying. Look I put in a good word for you and the guy was interested in meeting you."

"What's the job?"

Declan took another mouthful of lager. "Does it matter? It's a wage Marcus. It's better than signing on. At least you'll be earning enough to get out more than once every giro day."

"It's got to be crap if you're not keen on telling me what it is."

"Ok, it's in telesales."

Marcus shook his head. "Shit man, you're not serious? Not that con!"

"No honestly it's not what you think," Declan said trying to placate his friend. "The basic salary is decent. Really! Okay so you are on commission, but if you do alright then you're on a good whack."

"Yeah targets that mean you have to work like a slave," Marcus added sarcastically.

"Marcus this guy isn't like that."

"Ok. Selling what?"

"Holidays and insurance. It's a doddle, you'll do alright, believe me."

"I don't know."

"Well at least get in touch with him and see what he's got to say. What's to lose?"

"Yeah I suppose so," Marcus admitted reluctantly.

"Good man," Declan smiled as he handed Marcus a business card. "Don't forget to tell him that you know me and we've worked together."

Marcus shook his head. "You getting a fee or something?"

Declan smiled, finished the rest of his beer and got up. "I'll get another round in."

As he rose, three attractive young women, all in their early twenties, two white and one mixed-race, burst noisily into the pub. Their laughing and brazen manner immediately attracted both Declan and Marcus' attention.

Looking towards the women, Declan nodded his head. "They look fit."

"Okay I suppose," Marcus replied indifferently. He had already realised that the mixed-race woman was the same one he had seen get in the gold BMW.

"Listen to yourself. You're starting to sound like a sad loser mate. Get a life!" Declan ribbed.

High in Lambton House, Natasha closed the book and rubbed her tired eyes. That was enough studying for one night. What was called for was a hot bath and coffee. Some wind down music would be nice too. She could start with the music.

Natasha, now softer and more feminine in a white towelling gown was languorous with true physical tiredness. She wriggled off the narrow guest bed and fiddled with the knobs on the old radio set that had gathered dust on the little cabinet adjacent to her pillow.

"That's broken," Wendy, her father's partner, had told her ungraciously when she had first shown Natasha her allotted quarters. "Used to be Lisa's...." Wendy caught herself, "your mother's or you had it when you were little I gather. I was going to chuck it out, but your dad said you'd kick up a fuss."

Having scored a hit and made her point, Wendy remembered herself and adopted a more gracious manner. Kevin had a big thing about catfights. She mustn't be the obvious aggressor. "I don't suppose you'd like to take it with you to college?" she suggested, all helpful sweetness.

Natasha was neither a fool nor a complete pushover. "It's heavy," she said refusing to rise to the bait, "the retro look's back in fashion now and it's got a lovely tone. That's why mum was so fond of it. She had a really good musical ear. But I guess you never knew that." She felt better when Wendy turned and stormed off.

The crackling subsided as she managed to find Jazz FM and turned the volume down to a bare minimum.

Next, she braved the kitchen where her father would be getting himself a late night snack. Supper had been a gluey pasta affair and Kevin did not trust foreign food to see him through the small hours, so he was arduously fixing himself a sort of sandwich while his partner's back was turned. Wendy, from faint splashing and hissings, was in the shower and likely to be long. How much hot water would there be left for a bath Natasha mused. More to the point, could Wendy ever be really clean?

"Dad?"

"Hhhrrr"

"Mind if I get some cereals and a coffee?"

She was already reaching for the bowl and packet, nevertheless he tracked her movements with deep suspicion. Natasha was gaining a confidence that was beginning to slip from his grasp. The put-downs weren't keeping her in check the way they had used to do. They weren't ......effective. She was in a world of her own, shrugging them off, coming back here bold as brass whenever it suited her; slipping ten pound notes behind Wendy's fridge magnets to "pay for her keep".

"Hhhrr. Make sure you clear up after yourself then. I don't want Wendy slaving around with washing up round the clock just because you've decided to land on us for your holidays."

Father and daughter locked eyes that were alike. Kevin also had the same fine pale skin and thin bones. He too, for all his aggression, had been prey; Wendy's unrightful prey. They assessed each other. When he found that this strange, unregarded girl, who had once been his loving daughter, was looking at him with something like compassion, Kevin plunged his knife into the open jar of tuna sweet corn spread. Fuck compassion, she had better get off her high horse and learn to respect him again.

Marcus cursed at the clock, which read 12:30 p.m. He hadn't intended to sleep so late. He got out of bed, counted the mixture of notes and coins on the bedside table. The remains of his giro after he paid all his bills was a measly twenty-eight pounds and fifty pence, which he would have to try to make last until his next cheque. Thankfully he rarely went out and it cost nothing (especially as he hadn't yet paid his licence) to watch the television.

As he walked to the kitchen to put on the kettle, Marcus caught sight of the mixed-race woman from the pub. She was lighter than Maxine. Smoother, groomed solely to allure, but nevertheless cut from the same cloth.

The mere thought of Maxine caused him to wince. Would he ever get over her? Even though he had long since stopped thinking of her as his wife, (the divorce rather helped that) she still had the annoying habit of controlling his life. He wished he could stop thinking of her – period!

Marcus remained at the window watching the woman carrying items from the BMW into the expensive, upmarket building opposite. When, after she had not re-appeared for ten minutes, Marcus decided to settle down to watch TV.

He had just found the remote and was about to turn on the TV, when the muffled sound of arguing seeped through from the thin plasterboard walls of the flat next door. Marcus pressed the remote, and turned the volume up to listen to the host of the chat show introduce today's topic.

The programme was only a few minutes old when the doorbell rang. Remote in hand, he walked to the front door, checked through the spy hole where he saw the diminutive figure of Natasha biting her nails.

Marcus opened the door to his neighbour who was wearing a pair of red jeans and a loose cheesecloth top that had unintentionally been left unbuttoned to reveal a pair of firm breasts. She was not wearing any make-up and looked younger than her twenty-three years. She was obviously distressed.

"Look, I'm sorry to be a nuisance," she said apologetically.

"That's okay."

She bit on her lip sheepishly. "Can I come in please?"

"Sure," Marcus said, opening the door to allow her in.

"Are you alright? Would you like a cup of tea or coffee?" he offered sensing her need for company.

"Do you mind?"

"Don't be silly of course I don't. Have a seat," he said, showing her to the sofa before walking to the 'kitchen' area and switching on the kettle. "What would you prefer, tea or coffee?"

Natasha sat down and nervously nibbled away at her fingernails. What was she doing here? Did she seriously expect this man, who she had previously only had brief chats with, to take the time to listen to her woes. Why should he care?

"Tea please."

Marcus opened a cupboard and took out two mugs.

"I haven't seen you around much lately," he said, trying to break the nervous silence.

"I'm on mid-term break,"

There was a short pause before she continued. "I'm really sorry. I just had to get out of there."

13

"What happened?"

"Nothing really."

The whistling of the kettle as it finished boiling interrupted the conversation.

"Milk and sugar?"

"Milk and one sugar thanks."

Marcus made a cup of tea for Natasha and a coffee for himself. He handed her the mug and perched on the bed.

Natasha took a sip of the tea. It didn't take long before the flood banks burst and she let it all out.

"I just had to get out of there, but I didn't want to be on my own."

Marcus waited for her to explain.

"I can't stand her. She just loves rubbing my face in it."

"Who?"

"Her! *Wendy!*" It was almost a wail. "My dad's girlfriend. The bitch." She drank more of the tea. "My mum and dad got divorced because of her. You know something? People said my mother actually….." Natasha took a heaving breath, leaving the sentence incomplete. "I can't stand her."

There was a nervous pause while tension accrued and Natasha took herself in hand. Whatever Natasha's mother actually had or hadn't done, it definitely wasn't good.

"What are you studying?" Marcus asked patiently, trying to diffuse the situation.

"Biochemistry and Genetics."

"Right," Marcus answered, which led to another pause. "I'm impressed," he added, with the smallest possible muscle movement that could count as a smile.

"What do you do?" Natasha asked.

"I'm unemployed."

"Oh."

She finished her tea. Marcus picked up the empty mugs and placed them carefully in the sink. He checked his watch again.

"Look, I was going for a drink," Marcus lied.

"I'm sorry. I'll get going," said Natasha standing to leave.

"You don't have to go. I mean why don't you let me buy you a drink?"

"No I shouldn't have disturbed you."

"Please. You need to talk," Marcus said in a gentle persuasive voice. "Come on; let me buy you a drink."

14

"Are you sure?"

"Honest. Come on let's go."

"Okay then," Natasha smiled. Her turn to try. She wasn't sure how to talk about it.

She hadn't had any real friends when her mother died. She had shied away from counsellors later on at college. She was even reluctant to shame her father in public. Theirs had been such a family for not washing its dirty linen in public. Keeping up appearances.

For months after Natasha's dad had really gone to live with Wendy, her mother had kept up appearances to the extent of the washing she hung on the line: men's shirts. *Clean linen only.* Trying to fool the neighbours into thinking that her husband still lived there.

God knows why she had been so afraid of what people thought, Natasha reflected, drifting away from Marcus into her own private hell. All around their little terraced council house up the Angel, there had been fornication, partner swapping and adultery.

It was no different with the posh neighbours up the road and around the corner in the Canonbury Parks. They were luckier, because they could afford to hide behind proper blinds, not frilly nets and thin print curtains.

People from all the other maisonettes had been able to see Lisa's silhouette curled up on the couch; with drooping head and arms tight around a cushion, as if letting go of it might be the death of her. Lisa had shrunk from human contact, being too sensitive to bear the comment. She'd stopped going out, stopped opening the curtains; started taking anti-depressants, then a whole packet of anti-depressants, until the curtains closed permanently.

Marcus took a swig from his pint of lager and placed the Bacardi Breezer in front of Natasha as they finally found an empty table in the *Market Tavern.*

"Thanks. My dad says I'm being - unreasonable. He loves that word. He says it wasn't her fault; that they didn't mean for it to happen. I think that's crap. That's just an excuse for being selfish."

She took a nip of her drink whilst unconsciously twisting a strand of hair around her finger. Marcus allowed her to continue. It was obvious she needed to talk to someone and she had chosen him.

"How *can* a woman do that to another woman? She didn't care about anybody else, not my mother, not me. He's just as bad. They just thought about themselves."

"You don't have to tell me."

She didn't seem to hear him, and carried on. "Anyway, Mum became depressed and killed herself not long after, so I had to move in with them. They got away with it alright. The GP gave evidence at the inquest – they decided that it was Accidental Death or Misadventure because they said she was meant to be too ill and dopey to know what she was doing. I just played along, but I knew she deliberately killed herself."

"I should let you know I'm divorced," Marcus said quietly.

"I'm sorry. I shouldn't….. " Natasha apologised, still busy with the strand of hair.

"Don't be. I agree with you. My wife left me," he said, surprised that he was opening this still festering wound to someone he hardly knew.

It was now Marcus who was lost in thought, reliving past memories.

He stared at Maxine, wondering whether she had decided to do something a bit wicked but frivolous and expensive, like buying a house in Tangier. Something that would cause a big stir, but not a horror that would blow his soul apart he had hoped.

But that was not Maxine's style. No, she had taken a lover. Someone else! Had given him a month to vacate the house. Give her an address for her lawyers to contact she had ordered, triumphant, hateful, businesslike.

"Des and I need space to build our relationship with each other and our family." - the only explanation offered.

"Why?" he had asked, his mouth making a pitiful smiling shape (he knew now that was pure shock). It had put him off smiling. "Why? What have I done?" he had wanted to ask.

Then angry and self-righteous.

"Look, I'm not wasting my time explaining anything to you; if you don't get it then that's your problem. I've given you as much as I can and after all these years we're getting nowhere. You're a man in an insignificant job, with small goals and little ambition – I won't settle for that. I've told you before, my son and I deserve better and Des can offer us that. It's over, we're over – you get over it!"

"You know, I sometimes wonder if your parents didn't realise how inadequate you were and just wanted to get rid of their useless son."

And all he could think to say back was: "What did I do wrong?"

Natasha waited in silence, waiting until he could find the right words.

Marcus stirred again. "Yep, she left me."

Natasha's voice was normal, soft and direct.

"Why?"

"She found someone else," Marcus answered coldly. He finished his pint and gestured to her glass. "Do you want another?"

"I'll get them," Natasha offered.

"No I asked you. I'll get them," Marcus insisted.

Marcus picked up the glasses, made his way to the bar and bought another round of drinks then returned to the table and handed Natasha another bottle.

"Thanks," her fingers finally free from her hair.

"No problem," Marcus answered all normal again now that the subject had moved on. "How long have you been at university?"

"I'm in my second year."

"Right. What exactly are you studying?"

"Do you really want to know?"

"Of course."

"Well last year we studied the fundaments of cell biology, genetics and molecular structure. In layman's terms – how the body is put together and works."

"Seems too deep for me."

Natasha laughed; a soft quiet laugh. "Not exactly a winner at parties either. A bit like telling someone you play a musical instrument and then having to declare it's actually a bassoon."

Marcus let out a semblance of a laugh himself.

"Didn't you ever think of going to uni?"

Marcus shook his head. "I'm not really academic. I suppose I was never encouraged by my parents. They didn't see the point in me studying for a piece of paper when I could be out making money. That and being too busy running their errands and looking after them. To be honest school was just an escape from the chores for me.

"Are you involved with anyone?" Natasha asked casually as she fingered her hair nervously.

17

"No. How about you?" Marcus replied, wondering where that question had come from.

"No," she paused to sip her drink. "God we're a right pair of saddoes."

Marcus smiled. "You started it."

"Sorry," Natasha said, coiling the lock of her hair around her finger.

"You like that word don't you?"

"Sorry. I won't say it again," she said, looking down at her drink.

"Good."

"Am I bugging you?"

"No. Why, do I give you that impression?"

"I don't know I just wondered. I'm not always this boring you know."

"I never said you were boring."

As the mid-afternoon set in, the pub emptied. Natasha watched as the barman switched channels on the big, silent television slanted in the corner high above the bar. Her eyes widened at the sight of sweating men in bright vests leaping and straddling impossibly high bars, to fall sprawling backwards on great blocks of foam. Skinny girls, elbows working like pistons, paced and spurted around a track.

"Do you like sports?"

Natasha blushed, but her eyes glowed, "I like running. I used to run at school."

"Really?"

"Don't sound so shocked. I was quite good."

"I wouldn't have taken you for…. I mean you don't look like a runner."

"Well you're wrong. I used to run for the county."

"Why did you stop; if you were good enough to run for the county, you were obviously pretty good?"

"Don't know really," she replied, lowering her head and reaching for a strand of hair to twist. For a moment she remembered those days. Her achievements that had failed to impress either parent. It had been "That's good love," from her mother, and an indifferent "Don't know what you want all that exercise for. Do better stopping still and getting some meat on those bones," from her father. He

18

never dreamed that his comments could hurt, but when she had become self-conscious about her boobs; that had made him laugh. "Guess Mum's death put thing in perspective. I had more important things to do," she said sadly.

Marcus took a sip of his beer, feeling guilty for pressing the young girl who had retreated into herself again. The truth was he himself had truly excelled at the hurdles. Could have been an Olympic prospect his teacher had said, selection for the Junior National team and all the signs for the full squad had been a less-than-remote possibility if only he had been able to attend the after school training.

But of course there had been his parents disapproval and the Church. Ironically his fate had been decided when he'd injured his knee, had too many cortisone injections, lost interest and that had been that; career over before it started. Perhaps that was why he was beginning to warm to Natasha. In many ways despite the difference in years, they both had shared experiences. First time out with a girl for ages and he had managed to upset her. She didn't deserve that.

They fell to commenting on the performances on screen, following the competition, shared a plateful of 'homemade chunky chips' covered with ketchup; backed this or the other contestant. A Swede won the High Jump Gold, whilst a sandy-haired girl from the American Mid-West triumphed in her middle-distance heat, but looked thoroughly miserable about it.

"Imagine how you would feel if that was you winning a title? That still could be you, you're young enough. You should toughen yourself up, go for it," he said, hoping to cheer her up, yet wondering if he had phrased it right.

Natasha picked up her drink and for a moment saw the possibilities as she savoured the taste of the alcohol. Perhaps those few words were capable of opening a world of new possibilities.

The sports programme was followed by the News, with the sound off.

"What do you think they are talking about?" Marcus asked pointing to the screen where a couple of men seemed to be arguing. In the background, the logo of the lottery was plainly visible.

Natasha scrunched up her face, twirled her hair furiously round her finger as she thought. "Mmm, I think the smaller one is upset because when they bought the lottery ticket they agreed to share and

19

now that they've won the other bloke has denied any agreement and is claiming the money is his."

Marcus chuckled. "Very creative, but I bet that he is mad because their numbers came up and he forgot to buy a ticket."

"Not bad. But I am sure that the other guy, (who just happens to be his ex-lover) is suing him for taking the money for the ticket and spending it on hair removal treatment. "

They laughed, real laughs, until with the time after seven o'clock, they sadly ran out of money for drinks.

"Thanks for listening," Natasha said as they walked home.

"Anytime. You know you're welcome."

"Thanks. I really enjoyed today. Can I return the compliment?"

"What?"

"Can I buy you a drink tomorrow?"

"That's alright. You don't have to."

"I'd like to."

Marcus shrugged his shoulders. "Well it's up to you."

"Right, I'll see you tomorrow."

Natahsa waited for a few seconds before opening the door and going inside. Was it worth it – did she have *time* – to try out for the Uni Athletics Club? She could get subsidised kit, probably, if she made it into the squad. Still, even if she didn't join she could start using the track. Go running again.

Toughen herself up, as Marcus had told her. She was sure he had really meant more than just running. It was all part of the same process; taking charge of her life.

Natasha visualised Wendy wobbling around a track, and grinned as she slipped the key in the front door lock.

Chapter 3

Andrea Bailey rolled over in her empty bed. The silk sheets that covered it made a soft, protesting whisper in the process. She yawned lazily, rubbed her eyes before emerging naked from the king-sized bed and walked to the chair where she had neatly placed her silk bathrobe the night before.

She moved through to the bathroom, turned on both taps, added some bath salts and then picked up the two letters that stuck out of the letterbox on her way to the kitchen where she made herself a cup of Earl Grey tea. She sat herself down and opened the envelopes - both addressed to 'the occupier'. Andrea, deciding she was not interested in further credit cards or sponsoring a third world child, ripped them up and placed them in the bin. She would have been surprised had any personal mail found its way to this address.

When she had emptied her cup, Andrea returned to the bathroom, turned off the taps and let the bathrobe drop to the floor as she stretched one of her long, pale- chocolate legs into the bath. Satisfied with the temperature, Andrea lowered her body into the foamy liquid and felt the instant bliss as water rose to cover her hard brown breasts.

She picked up the soap (Appassionata by Laura Bugotti) and turned it slowly between her wet palms until the lather was creamy and pungent. Then she stroked it down her arms, across her breasts down, down, to the tips of her crimson-tipped toes. As she worked she conducted her routine inventory. Toe nails: still flawless. No action needed. The skin of her calves: moisturiser. Finger nails: wrong shade for today's outfit. A duskier, subtler, tint to complement a plum-coloured, raw silk trouser suit; think orchid she murmured to herself, and smiled at her own absurdity. She was a professional, not an airhead.

Although she usually enjoyed lazing in her bath, Andrea was aware that today she had to be on the road early. She quickly washed, stepped out of the bath, and dried herself in an ivory towelling kimono, which she wrapped around herself before padding barefoot back to her bedroom.

She sat in front of the dressing table, and turned this way and that into the mirror as she carefully and surely perfected her daytime make-up. Andrea never compromised.

Once she had finished her make-up, Andrea dressed, grabbed her bag and made her way out of Napier Court. She used the remote to open the door of the BMW and started the engine. Knowing she had lots to do today, Andrea decided her first stop was the flat in Chiswick. For a moment, she even contemplated making a detour to Hackney.

Natasha took a last look in the mirror before closing the door to her bedroom and leaving the flat. She had put on a little make-up and had done her hair. First she had tried pinning it up, as her Indian friend did – one slide, or even a biro, holding up a whole great twist. But Natasha's hair slipped free of the single mooring, so she had brushed it down and pinned the slide in just to look pretty.

The make up came in a little jade-green case and was a cute set of miniature cream-colour blocks complete with applicators, brush and mirror. It was airport duty-free booty; a 'gift' that came when you bought a fair sized bottle of big-brand, full-strength perfume. A holiday souvenir from the chief barmaid at *The Old Spotted Mare* in Nottingham, where Natasha pulled pints on a Friday night. "Get a bit of lippy on, love," Yvette had said. "Here's a starter kit from sunny Florida. You couldn't call it showy. No one'll call you a slapper. Its classy stuff, this. Clinique."

She was pleased that the pair of candy striped trousers and tight tee shirt showed off her figure – not that she expected to be complimented for her body; in fact, she could not recall anyone **ever** telling her she had a nice body.

Well not exactly true, perhaps the words may have been uttered during the few sexual encounters she had endured. The one 'steady' relationship, (which had lasted all of four weeks and ended when Alex had drunkenly told her that the reason he wanted her was for convenient sex, not love) had taught her that words were too often used by some men solely to flatter until they got you between the sheets.

Natasha was more than confident that her slender figure would never attract such comments as "God her bum looks big in that!" In fact she was more than conscious of her unimpressive backside and any means of enhancing that region was welcome."

She took a deep breath before knocking on Marcus' door, hoping that he was in.

It seemed like an age before he opened the door dressed in jeans and a slightly creased blue polo shirt.

"Hi. Ready for that drink?" she asked, thankful that he was indeed home.

"Right. I'll just grab a coat."

Marcus disappeared inside, turned off the TV and picked up a wine-coloured blouson from behind the door before joining Natasha. They completed the three-minute walk to the *Market Tavern* in a nervous silence.

"What are you having?" Natasha asked Marcus as a middle-aged barmaid approached.

"A pint of lager please."

"A pint of lager and a vodka and orange please," she repeated to the barmaid who was already fetching glasses.

The barmaid served Natasha, politely accepted her twenty-pound note for the drinks, deposited the note in the till then gave her the change.

Although the pub was busy as usual, they managed to find an empty table and sat down.

Natasha started to clear the tabletop. She dumped the empty crisp packet into the ashtray, stacked the two half-empty glasses and blew some spilt ash carefully onto a discarded paper serviette. Finally, she picked up all the clutter calmly, with practised ease, and left them at the end of the bar before threading her way back.

Lust had started to stir in Marcus when Natasha had bent over the table, pursing her lips to blow away the miniature mound of ash, but he wasn't ready to relax and enjoy it.

I'm turning into a dirty old man. How old is she? How old am I? Marcus thought.

"Feeling a bit better today?" he asked.

"Yes. Sorry about yesterday."

Marcus tutted, "I thought you weren't going to keep on apologising."

"Right."

"What's it like at university?"

"Bloody hard work."

"Is it?"

"Too right. It's not the coursework; I can cope with that. It's the fact that I've got to work in order to get by."

"What kind of work do you do?"

"I work in a restaurant and do some cleaning in a small hotel. Boring really, but it means I can finish my course." She paused to take a drink. "What about you? What do you usually do?"

"Me, I used to work in an insurance office."

"What happened?"

"I was made redundant. The company got taken over and the new firm decided it needed to 'downsize'."

Natasha finished her drink and signalled to Marcus. "Drink up."

Marcus waved his hand, "I'll get these."

"No. I told you it was my turn tonight." She waited for him to finish before taking the glasses.

"I'll give you a hand."

Natasha struck a self-assured pose. "Keep the seats. I think I can manage to carry two drinks."

Marcus watched as she made her way to the bar. What was it about her that had caused him to open up to her? He had grown used to being alone, safe in the solitude of his own company where no one could harm him. Now he was having conversations; expressing feelings he had kept to himself for so long.

He heard her voice before he realised that she had returned.

"Do you mind if I ask you something personal?" Natasha asked nervously as she placed the pint glass in front of Marcus.

"Thanks," he said accepting the drink, "I won't know until you ask."

"You don't have to answer if you don't want to."

"Go for it."

Natasha sipped her drink. "How long ago did you split up from your wife?"

"Nearly two years now."

"What happened to her?"

"She's living with the bloke."

"Does she live close by?"

"No. She lives in our old house in Essex."

Natasha bit pensively on her lips before asking, "Do you still see her?"

"No I don't," Marcus answered quickly, with no attempt to disguise the malice in his voice.

"Why did you move to Blackheath? It's such a long way from Essex. Have you got family around here?"

Marcus was relieved when the conversation was interrupted by the arrival of three well-dressed women wearing expensive designer clothes, who raucously entered the pub and approached the bar.

The loud pop of the champagne cork caught Marcus and Natasha's attention.

"Looks like they're having a good time."

"The mixed-race one lives in Napier Court."

Natasha raised her eyebrows, "Alright for some."

"What do you think she does for a living?"

Natasha shrugged her shoulders, "How should I know?"

"Have a guess," he urged.

Natasha picked up her glass and traced the rim with her finger as she studied the group. "Something well paid. Advertising or marketing?"

"What makes you think that?"

"Well, they don't look like professionals such as lawyers or doctors, but they can afford authentic designer clothes. I used to work Saturdays in a posh boutique and I can tell that what they are wearing doesn't come cheap. So am I right?"

"I don't know. It was bugging me."

"Then why don't you just ask her?" said Natasha, a little jealous that he obviously found the woman attractive.

"It doesn't matter. I just wondered that's all. I thought she might be a model or an actress, someone famous."

"I suppose she could be. I don't recognise her though."

"She doesn't work regular office hours."

"How do you know?"

"I've seen her coming out of her building in the afternoons when I go to sign on."

Another cork popped as the women opened another bottle of champagne.

Natasha leant forward and said in a low voice, "Perhaps she's a prostitute, or a drug dealer."

"What makes you say that?"

"Well think about it. Irregular hours, flash clothes and expensive apartment; obvious isn't it."

"A bit too stereotypical though isn't it?"

Natasha took a sip of her drink. "Some of the girls at my college strip or - well, you know. Do it for money. "

"Why?"

She shook her head in disbelief. "Why do you think? It's quick money that gets them out of debt."

"A bit drastic. You'd think that someone clever enough to go to university would be able to manage their finances," Marcus said unsympathetically.

Natasha leaned forward, forearms on the table, risking pools of spilt drink. Her eyes shone bright with animation; remembering how she used to run. How her heart had pounded as she picked up speed, then settled again as she maintained the acceleration and her body adjusted to the new demands: effort remembered; effort sustained. The athlete was back.

"Yes, but it's easy to see why. When mum died, I had to work full time for a year and save all my wages to make sure I could get through my first year at Uni. My dad didn't help me one bit."

"I watched this talk show on TV about people who did things others didn't approve of for money. They called them guests, but they had to disguise the faces and put their voices through synthesisers. They had burglars, prostitutes and drug dealers. There was even a murderer, you know a hit man," said Marcus.

"Sounds like a nice bunch."

"That's what I thought at first, but when I heard them explaining why they did what they did, I almost found myself understanding them."

"What?" exclaimed Natasha in horror, "How could they justify killing someone?"

"I don't know. The girls at college who strip or whatever, what do you think about them?"

"I don't know them personally. I'm too busy getting by the legal ways; well apart from taking a bit of cash in hand. I understand the pressure they are under and how it might seem to be an easy way out, but it isn't is it?"

"No, but you understand and you don't judge them, that's what I meant."

"Yes, but just because you understand doesn't make it right. I couldn't do what they do." She finished her drink and stood up. "Last one - and I'm buying."

Marcus held his hands up in resignation. Natasha smiled and left for the bar.

As Natasha reached the counter, one of the three smartly dressed young women, shimmied up to Marcus' table. She - like her friends - definitely rated as a "Babe", a girl who would always, always find time and money for leg waxes and hair highlights.

"Do you know where the ladies are?" she asked, without faint pretence.

"Yes, they're just around the corner in the other bar," Marcus answered.

"No they're not – we're over there," she said pointing to her two friends who were waving and laughing.

"We're *real* ladies," she winked and gestured to the chair beside him. "My name's Hannah. Is that seat taken?"

"Afraid so," Marcus said and nodded at Natasha who was returning with the drinks.

Hannah bent over and made sure Marcus got an eyeful of her ample bosoms that were bursting out of the low cut top. "Well if you get bored, you know where we are." She smiled, touched-fingers suggestively with the tips of her short blonde hair, swivelled back to her friends, smiling at Natasha as she sashayed past her.

Marcus smiled as he watched her exaggerated strut, buttocks swaying invitingly. Under his breath he spat out, "Fucking slut!"

Natasha put down the drinks. "I wasn't interrupting anything was I?" she ribbed.

"No you bloody well weren't," Marcus snarled.

Sensing the change in Marcus' mood, Natasha sat quietly and played with her hair as she waited for him to start a conversation. There was no charge of attraction now in his looks or manner. The three women had spoilt it.

Like those vampire sisters in Dracula, Natasha thought, remembering how, aged twelve, she'd read Dracula – the proper novel – sitting demurely, schoolgirl knees together, in a shiny armchair at her local library, almost until closing time. When the dowdy-but-nice lady on the desk came up behind her to announce discreetly that it was ten to seven, she had actually shrieked.

Natasha looked apprehensively at him over the rim of her glass and wondered what she had done to upset him. Any further attempts to instigate dialogue were met with muted response by Marcus who for some unknown reason was now clearly brooding.

It was with some relief mixed with trepidation that the evening ended and Marcus walked Natasha to her flat.

"Thanks for the drinks," Marcus said as he fished into his pockets for his keys.

"We're even now".

"I wasn't keeping tally," Marcus snapped.

"I didn't mean it like that," Natasha said defensively.

Marcus detected the hurt in her voice. "I'm sorry. It's okay. Look feel free to knock again if you want anything."

"Are you sure?" she asked tentatively.

He nodded.

She smiled, "You might regret saying that."

"I don't think I will."

"Thanks. Goodnight then."

"Bye."

Marcus walked across his bed-sit to the fridge, took out a cold can of lager and tugged on the ring pull. He selected a cassette, inserted it into the video. Placing his lager on the bedside table, he lay on the bed and pressed the remote.

He remained riveted to the screen watching the talk show that he had described to Natasha. Marcus fast-forwarded to a guest who was describing her early life in a run down project in America. She recounted her story of her introduction to wealthy men, and how she had no qualms about dating married men.

Marcus' face contorted with hatred when the host asked how she felt about her actions and the guest flicked back her hair, smiled before saying "Sometimes you've just got to do what you have to in order to get what you want."

Fit women, beautiful women; what they did to you with their cheers, their sobs, and their long-festered grievances brewing in those heaving bosoms. They could always *justify* why they do what they did. Take you for all you had, everything you had given, your own roof from over your head and even your children. That was what they did; just as his mother had, just as Maxine had. Get a life? More like take a life?

Marcus pressed the rewind button on the remote and played the clip once; then again and again.

Chapter 4

Claudia St Clair sat on a chair in the dining room of her home. The West Indian and African art that they had painstakingly sought out over many years were thoughtfully sited about the well-decorated deep carpeted and long draped room that was Claudia's pride and joy.

Now thirty-five years old, Claudia was a woman with presence; matriarch material ahead of the surplus bodyweight required of the role. At this time of her life, she was shapely, toned from the gym and with slight threatenings of over-muscularity around the shoulders and thighs. Not especially tall, there was already a hint of stockiness. She would never lack grace, because her head was so elegantly set, back and up, with a proud flared nose and lifted chin. Her smooth skin was darker than caramel, almost charcoal in the hollows of her face. Large expressive eyes with brows permanently arched, as if tautened by her hair which was drawn straight back and up from her face.

Beside her at the table sat an impeccably dressed, well-groomed, light-skinned black man of thirty-eight. The expensive made-to-measure suit showed that Ken St Clair was exactly what he appeared; a highly successful businessman.

Seated around the table with them were three couples. The gathering consisted of a black male in his forties with a flourish in his manner suggestive of an up-and-coming barrister and his thirty-something partner. Theirs was the glamour of successful professionals: good shoes, good haircuts. The woman was also black; her jewellery was platinum, and little enough of it. Her shirt was grey silk; a black woollen mid-length skirt completed the ensemble of work clothes, slightly creased from the efforts of a stressful day in the Public Relations Department of a government office.

The other black male, Dr Franklyn Beaupierre, a Senior ENT Registrar at Guys and St Thomas', was accompanied by a blonde (dark roots just starting to show through Claudia noted) white female in her mid to late twenties from Physiotherapy, who whilst being suitable eye candy, did not realise the extent of unease she had brought to the gathering.

The third couple was white, both around thirty-six years old. University friends of Ken, they ran their own successful E-Business from home in Battersea. They took turns texting the nanny to check on their three-year-old daughter Kitty. The woman looked weary, but she had found time to change into a sleeveless, fairly pricey, little black dress from Zara. The man, on the other hand, was dressed smart-casual, soft, floppy fair hair, rather defiantly househusband, non-corporate, and suede shod. Claudia wondered if they had consulted before dressing to go out.

Ken St Clair stood and tinkled his crystal glass with a spoon.

"My dear friends you all know you have been *summoned* here in this fashion for a reason."

Laughter from the others caused a brief interruption before he continued. Claudia smiled politely.

"So, I am *charged* with announcing to you, you select band of few; that my darling wife Claudia has been selected for promotion to the auspicious rank of Detective Chief Inspector."

"Well done Claudia."

"Congratulations."

"About time."

"Brilliant news."

Ken lifted his hand and quietened the volley of compliments before he continued. "So dear friends let us drink a toast in celebration and in appreciation of her wonderful news," he said and raised his glass, "To the soon to be Detective Chief Inspector Claudia St Clair."

The guests stood and repeated the toast before breaking out into a chorus of "For she's a jolly good fellow."

Claudia took their congratulations and good wishes gracefully; even if she was slightly miffed that not only had Ken neglected to invite even one of *her* colleagues to this surprise, but also had not managed to prevent Dr Beaupierre from bringing his preposterously young bit of stuff to their home. She would let him know her feelings on that later.

Ever the diplomat, Claudia smiled sweetly as the blonde-haired woman kissed the doctor. Too pretty, too young.

Marcus woke with a yawn, found the remote that he had left on the bedside table, turned on the TV and zapped through the channels until he found a chat show. The female host announced that the theme of today's programme was women and their changing role in today's society.

Eyes entranced by the procession of female guests, Marcus sat up a little more in the bed. He listened as the first guest stated that she does not want a man in her life. She explained that if she wants sex, then, "I go out and have me a one-night stand." She added that it was her right to decide what she did with her body and if men did not like it – tough!

"Fucking slag!"

The next guest announced that she is a single mother who had returned to work eight weeks after giving birth; that her child was well looked after in a crèche and had not suffered. She explained that apart from conception, the father had been of no use to her. She hadn't told him she was pregnant and was better off without him.

"Bitch," Marcus shouted loudly over the applause from the TV audience. Is that what men had become now; mere toys for females, to be disposed of as and when pleased, he reflected.

The final guest was a woman who stated she had been a battered wife who finally flipped and killed her husband in a moment of rage. When she revealed that she had received a sentence of probation, the audience applauded approvingly.

"Fucking cow! She kills a man and they cheer. What if that was a man? They would lock him up for life! Fucking bitches! Fucking bitches!" he ranted to himself.

Natasha eyed the numerous varieties of trainers with unease. She had consciously chosen to go to a specialist running shop to get proper advice in order to make an informed decision. If she was going to spend her hard-earned cash on something, then she was not going to be frivolous and squander it.

Then she remembered the old shop, where she had found her bargains in her school days, in return for helping to tidy up at closing time. In fact, Bernie, the proprietor, had offered her a Saturday job; but her Mum had been so fragile by then. Not well enough to leave.

The owner liked her because even though she had a quiet voice, she had been a good listener and a quick learner. If the shop had gone, so be it. But ... but ...what if he was still there, and she had to explain about her mother dying? Natasha frowned in her dilemma, before pulling herself together. So she would just tell him, wouldn't she?

A twenty-minute bus ride brought her to the old familiar shop, looking much the same as it had done seven years ago. On the display rack in the store's porch she fingered the price tag on a pair with massively built up soles and a pretty pink and silver flash. Was she looking at high fashion or high function? They would hardly take them back once she had tried them out for ten or so miles and found them wanting, would they?

The customers inside were mainly young, black and male; assessing racks of vests that did or did not hold the body heat, or expel moisture, or control airflow or support muscles. When they thought she wasn't looking, they assessed Natasha too.

At the counter, she asked after Bernie – who had not retired, but was now running a second branch two miles away the pleasant female assistant explained. Thirty-five minutes later, Natasha exited the shop smiling proudly as she carried her aptly chosen purchases. Not just shoes, a complete running kit for under £50! She had also left a message for Bernie, and felt that a friendship was halfway to being renewed.

Marcus stood by the window watching as the mixed-race woman from the block opposite pulled up in her BMW. He breathed heavily, still furious at the guests who had so proudly boasted of what he perceived as loathing of men.

A middle-aged man dressed in a stylish suit emerged from the passenger seat, walked round and opened the door to allow the mixed-race woman out of the car. He took her arm and together they entered Napier Court. Marcus remained transfixed. To his surprise after a short while, she reappeared at a window almost directly opposite his and drew the curtains closed.

As if spellbound, Marcus continued watching for a further hour until the couple finally materialized at the entrance to Napier Court then got in the car and drove off.

Marcus went to the kitchen, made himself some noodles then returned to the window. He proceeded to eat the paltry meal whilst keeping his watch on the block.

Andrea sang along with the tape, turned the BMW into the underground garage and eased into her parking space. Her black high heels made a noisy clicking sound as she walked towards the entrance to the flat. Yes, this was her real flat – a place unknown to others – where she could keep her secrets. Not that keeping your secrets was difficult in London; it was the perfect place for those who wanted anonymity, a city where people kept themselves to themselves; where no one bothered to ask questions. She grinned at the thought that none of her neighbours even knew that Thérèse Williams was her adopted name.

Andrea was just about to open the door to the flat when her mobile rang. She delved into her bag, found the phone and answered the call. She turned around and walked back to her BMW.

Marcus chewed restlessly on his nails. It was another three hours before the woman returned. This time she was with another man; again a suited middle-aged man. They followed her previous routine of withdrawing into her apartment, staying there for about an hour before coming out, getting into the BMW and driving off.

He finally gave up his vigil and returned to watching yet another chat show on TV. This was a more raucous American programme where all the guests were women about to tell their partners that they are having affairs.

He thought back to that day when his world had been destroyed. He remembered the feeling of shock, anger and hatred as he had opened the door.

Tears started to trickle from his eyes at the recollection of Maxine throwing his clothes unceremoniously out of the window onto prickly cotoneaster shrubs in the bed beneath; ("the best crime deterrent and anti-burglar device known to the police") said the leaflet from their Neighbourhood Watch Liaison Officer. Shouting obscenities at him as his young son looked on from the bedroom they had recently decorated together in the colour of his favourite football team.

Marcus became aware of the audience on the TV chat show cheering wildly as an attractive blonde woman announced to her husband that she had been cheating on him with his best friend.

The audience became even more animated as the 'best friend' was brought on stage and a fight between the two men commenced. Once they had been separated and calmed down, the woman added that she has also been seeing a woman.

Marcus could no longer contain his anger and disgust. His face twisted into a look of near insanity. He rose angrily, switched off the TV and went back to the window.

It was getting dark when the BMW pulled up and the mixed-race woman, accompanied by a pretty blonde, carried their expensive looking bags from the car. Marcus watched silently, his heart pounding as the lights came on in her flat before she again closed the curtain to him.

Chapter 5

Marcus wasn't quite sure when the idea had come to him, but once the notion had formed he found that it would not leave his head, and the more he thought about it, the more vindicated he felt. She had such a fucking easy life. If she could afford to live in Napier Court, maintain a BMW and dress in designer clothes; then she must have serious money. Money that she would not miss but which he needed – no deserved. Why shouldn't he have his life back?

He had watched her persistently for several days now. The fact that she only appeared to stay in the flat around three days a week was puzzling. Marcus knew he needed to know when she was likely to be around. One thing was sure; he could not rob her during the daytime. Not only was she was always coming and going; there was also the increased likelihood of being noticed.

However, whenever the woman (whose name he still did not know), stayed over at Napier Court, she had been out most nights for at least three hours. Marcus polished off the Jacob's cream cracker, wiped his hand across his lips to remove any remaining crumbs and checked his watch before leaving the window ledge. It had now been ten minutes since she had left the flat. He had enough time. He had to act now or he never would.

Hopefully the time he had used up watching those police crime programmes that inadvertently gave away clues as to what not to do when committing a crime, would now prove well spent. He had already picked out a pair of old jeans, a dark top and an old pair of trainers; all of which he would not miss when they were disposed of later.

Once he had finished dressing, Marcus selected a blank video cassette, inserted it into the video and set the programmer. He picked up a pair of the kitchen gloves he normally used to clean meat, stuffed them in his pocket and left the bed-sit.

He crossed the road, steeled himself as he feigned using the intercom and slipped in through the door unnoticed as a tenant left the building. He climbed the stairs quickly, but purposefully.

As he reached the third floor, Marcus neared a door that was partly open. He could hear male voices. He cautiously moved forward to sneak a quick look and saw two decorators in white overalls with their brushes in hand painting the walls of the flat. With two quick strides, he moved past the door and started up to the next level. He placed his foot on the wooden floor, which gave a noticeable squeak that caused him to flutter.

Marcus thought of taking a glance backward to see if he had been heard, but realising it would seem more suspicious, he boldly continued walking towards his destination, unaware that the younger of the two painters had caught a fleeting glimpse of his outline.

He turned left, walked past the first two doors and noticed that there were no lights on. Reaching into his pockets, he took out the gloves and donned them on hands that were starting to sweat. He knocked softly on the door and waited, pressing flat against the wall, out of view of any unexpected prying eyes that might look over the railings above.

He waited a short while before knocking again, this time a little louder. There was still no response. He approached the door and took a close look at it. Running a gloved hand over the frame, he tested it with his shoulder and was relieved to see it had sufficient give. He removed the phone card from his back pocket, ran it down the top of the frame until it met the lock. He leant against the door and on the third attempt, the lock popped open noiselessly.

Once inside the darkened apartment, Marcus took a minute for his eyes to become accustomed to the dimness then made his way to the window and drew the heavy velvet curtains before switching on the light.

The large living room was tastefully and expensively decorated. A large rug covered a beautiful polished natural wood floor. Marcus did not know whether the signed prints that adorned the wall were authentic or not. He picked up a Capo di Monte figurine, then what appeared to be an expensive vase, which he inspected before carefully replacing them.

He browsed through the large collection of CDs that were stored in alphabetical order. There had to be over three hundred discs. He shook his head enviously as he found some recent titles that he would have bought himself had he been able to afford them.

Marcus moved through to the kitchen, which was decked out with oak fittings. He opened cupboards which were full of tins and packets, then looked inside a fridge that was filled with smoked salmon, steaks, king prawns and caviar.   Marcus found a knife, cut some of the Roquefort cheese and made himself a sandwich with the thick fresh bread that he found in the fancy breadbin.

Beside the fridge were three empty bottles of champagne beside a newly opened box.

"Fucking spoiled bitch," Marcus said as he opened a bottle of lukewarm champagne and began necking it as he moved through to the bedroom.

The enormous bed was covered with silk sheets.   Huge frames holding erotic art hung on each wall.   He opened the walk-in wardrobe, found it full of designer clothes, many still brand-new, and covered in plastic.

On top of the bedside table, he saw a jewellery box.   When he flipped open the top, he noticed a platinum thumb ring, picked it up and had a quick look before putting it back then emptying the contents into the black backpack.

Warming to his task, Marcus opened the top drawer of a dresser. His eyes lit up at the sight of the expensive lingerie; again many brand new in unopened boxes. He tossed its contents onto the bed, picked up a purple silk teddy and softly traced it against his cheek before adding it to the heap on the bed.

Andrea slowed the BMW and easily manoeuvred it into her allocated parking space. She switched off the music and got out of the car with Michelle - effortlessly locking the doors behind her with the zapper and headed towards the building.

Marcus began rummaging through another drawer. As he tossed the neatly folded cashmeres and cardigans onto the bed unceremoniously, he felt a strange sensation; a mixture of power and satisfaction as the champagne started to work on his empty stomach. From now on, every time he saw her, he would remember this night.

Then bingo. He felt the packages under some T-shirts. There were several jiffy envelopes. He ripped one neatly open and smiled at the sight.

Michelle moved behind Andrea, ran her hand over her buttocks whilst nibbling an ear as Andrea pressed the button and waited for the lift.

"Not here," Andrea scolded as the blonde leant forward in an attempt to kiss her, the strong smell of brandy evident on Michelle's breath. This flat was for work not pleasure. She had chosen it because it was in such an ideal area, a place where no one would take notice of the comings and goings of seemingly wealthy men. Her rule had always been six months then move on.

Perhaps it would be better if in future she brought Michelle to Chiswick. Eventually she was going to have to decide whether Michelle was more than just a fling. It would mean trusting her; and trust was not something that came easily to Andrea.

Marcus finished the champagne, placed the jiffy envelopes in the rucksack and moved back to the kitchen where he washed the bottle before placing it beside the other empties then crossed to the living room.

"Shit," he uttered on peeking out of the window and seeing the gold BMW parked in its usual place. How long had it been back he wondered. He hurried across to the front door and switched off the light.

Andrea and Michelle got out of the lift and approached the front door. Michelle pressed Andrea against the door and hungrily kissed her whilst she looked through her bag for her keys.

"I want you so much," the blonde slurred; looking through glazed eyes as she pinned Andrea against the door and snaked a hand down her pants. Andrea brought out the keys and tried to find the lock as the drunken woman pawed at her. She pulled away and managed to turn the key in the lock.

Marcus stepped inside the storage cupboard, leaving it very slightly ajar. He heard the key turn in the lock followed by the slamming of the door and the sound of footsteps. The mixed-race woman appeared and tossed her bag down then turned and started kissing her blonde friend as they undressed each other hurriedly. Marcus felt himself getting excited as he watched tongue on breast and the urgency in the women increase.

They disappeared from his restricted view. It was only a matter of seconds before the sound of loud music came from the bedroom. Marcus breathed a huge sigh of relief that in the few moments before the women had entered the flat he had gathered the clothes and stuffed them under the bed.

He waited for what seemed an eternity before deciding that he would try to sneak out of the flat. He cautiously stepped from his hiding place, pressed his ear to the bedroom door and listened for a moment to the sounds coming from the within before crossing to the kitchen where he picked up a fresh bottle of champagne and headed for the door.

He turned ready to make good his escape when the door to the bedroom opened and the naked figure of the mixed-race woman emerged from the bedroom on her way to the bathroom. Marcus was transfixed by the sight.

"What the fuck are you doing in my flat?" she challenged.

She took a step towards him. Marcus could only stare at her nakedness, her beautiful firm breasts and her neatly shaven pussy.

"Who the hell are you?" she said squaring up to him. "I'm going to kill you, you wanker!"

She aimed a punch at him, which he dodged. She swung again, this time catching him on the shoulder.

In that instant she became Maxine, taunting him, making him feel inadequate. The contact sparked Marcus into action as instincts took over. He was not going to allow himself to get caught. He took a firm hold of the champagne bottle and brought it down with brutal force over her head.

The woman buckled and blood trickled from her head.

"You fucking black bastard!"

She charged into him, punching wildly. Marcus raised the bottle once more and hit her, stopping her in her tracks. He hit her again and this time she raised her hands and tried to deflect the blows as their effects started to take their toll.

"Please stop," Andrea pleaded as the fight left her and she realised the danger she was in.

Marcus brought the bottle down one final time and the woman at last dropped to the floor like a rag doll. He bent down and was about to check her pulse when he realised his gloved hand was covered in blood. He withdrew his hand and was getting up when the blonde came out of the bedroom in a sleepy, drunken state.

Before she was aware of what was happening, Marcus raised the bottle and repeatedly brought it down on his paralysed victim until the bottle smashed and shards of glass lay embedded in her bloody, pulpy mess of a skull. There was no need to check whether this one was dead. He went to the bathroom, ran his gloved hands under the tap until all the blood had gone, then dried them on a towel which he crumpled into the backpack before leaving the flat and apartment block unobserved and stepping into the reassuring darkness of night.

Once inside his bed-sit, he locked the door behind himself in relief. He went to the mirror and saw the blood that had splashed all over his clothes. What had she made him do?

He opened the backpack, tossed the jewellery and jiffy envelopes onto the bed and fetched a black bin liner from the 'kitchen' cupboard.

He stripped off slowly and carefully, making sure not to transfer the blood to any surfaces as he put each item of clothing into the bin liner. He stepped under the shower and remained there washing himself until the water turned icy cold.

After drying himself off with an old towel, which he tossed in the bin liner, Marcus sat down on the bed and stared at his reflection in the mirror. It had not been his fault.

"Shit! Shit! Shit!" he cursed.

He remained shivering naked on the bed, staring into the mirror for an age. He thought of all those crime programmes he watched late at night when he couldn't sleep for thinking of his son. He knew he had to think carefully, meticulously. It was her fault.

Finally, he stood up, searched in the drawers for a pair of scissors and carefully began snipping the clothes and towels into small shreds. He placed the strips of cloth into the metal waste bin, opened the window, then poured some of the white spirit he had removed from the kitchen cupboard into the bin and set it alight.

After repeating the process three times, he had to allow the bin to cool down. The bed-sit stunk, but Marcus continued until all the clothes were ashes. No chance of the bloodstained clothes being found now. He emptied the contents into another bin liner and placed it by the door.

He ripped open the jiffy bags and removed all the cash. He didn't bother to count the money. He gathered up the jewellery and placed it with the cash, which he put in a carrier bag, then wrapped into a tight plastic bundle.

Still naked, Marcus went in the shower again, shivering under the cold water. Why had she returned? he asked himself.

In the neighbouring flat Natasha lay awake listening to the sounds of jazz coming from the old radio, her mind unable to get Marcus out of her thoughts. Was there any chance that he might be interested in her? Whilst she had no problem with his colour, for all she knew, he might not date white women.

Marcus walked the deserted early morning, thankful that there were only a few workers about. A dustcart slowly made its way down the quiet street. The dustmen were enthusiastically going about their work and did not see Marcus as he walked behind the cart and tossed in the black bag containing the ashes that were once his clothes.

He carried on walking until he got to the car park. The derelict site had been earmarked for improvement under the Council's Centre Development Scheme to boost the borough's economy. Pending the launch of Phase 4, the car park that had once offered shoppers and workers budget parking, had been largely neglected and now served as an ideal shooting gallery for destitute drug users. The pair of mechanical ticket machines were often out of order and the set of recycling bins for Glass, Paper and Cardboard regularly set alight by bored youths.

Having checked the car park out when he had decided to rob the brash woman from Napier Court, he knew how to bypass the solitary, poorly positioned CCTV camera.

Marcus climbed the stairs, counting each floor in his head. He found the loose bricks that had taken him an age to prise out on his nightly visits and removed them slowly. He took out the plastic bundle from under his jacket, stuffed it in the empty cavity then carefully replaced the bricks.

His mission completed, Marcus started walking back home. As he turned into Jellicoe Street, he passed a young man in white overalls who nodded at him politely, crossed the road and entered Napier court.

Chapter 6

Lydia Thompson sat in front of the dressing table mirror applying her make-up. She was wearing a lacy bra and a pair of well-cut trousers. She picked up her mobile phone and dialled a stored number. Lydia let it ring for about three minutes before giving up and switching it off. She finished her make-up, put on a blouse and grabbed a jacket on her way out.

Natasha wrapped the bathrobe around her warm, freshly bathed body. She walked to her room, closed the door and perched on the bed. After the first few efforts that had left her sick, exhausted and aching, Natasha had re-discovered the pure pleasure she got from running. It was the one area of her life that she could be delightfully selfish about and not feel bad.

She caught her reflection in the mirror. One selfish thought led to another. She looked at her still damp hair, softly clinging, moulded around her shapely head and gracefully turned neck after its comb-through. Tendrils clung to her shoulders. It looked rather nice. It made her look like a mermaid.

It had been a long time since she had treated herself to a hairdo. A restyling in the kind of salon where they gave you fancy magazines to flick through while you waited for Deborah, Maureen, or (she suppressed a giggle) Natasha – anyway, the senior stylist - to come and consult about the glamorous new look you expected she would achieve.

Maybe it was time for a re-vamp to complement her newfound self-confidence. Not just cheap old 'The Salon', her usual resort, where you paid little, but were charged extra if you wanted your freshly washed and shorn locks to be dried as well as snipped.

No somewhere a bit upmarket. Gently towelling as she mused, Natasha recalled the salon she had loped past towards the end of today's run, when she was winding down her pace and noticing her surroundings in detail. It hadn't been ultra posh, but through the window gleamed black and white fixtures, lozenge-shaped mirrors, and a notice stating 'APPOINTMENTS NOT NECESSARY ON MONDAYS AND WEDNESDAYS'.

She checked the watch she had slipped off her wrist and left on her bedside table. What did she have to lose?

Lydia spotted the gold BMW outside Napier Court and pressed the buzzer for Andrea's flat. When there was no response, she walked back, looked up to see that the curtains to the flat were drawn closed. She took her mobile out of her bag and pressed the redial button. After a couple of minutes, she gave up. She opened her bag, tossed the phone inside, removed a set of keys and let herself in the outer doors. She took the lift to Andrea's flat, inserted the key, turned the lock and opened the front door.

"Andrea, where are you?" she called out.

Lydia walked inside, spotted the naked chocolate body and immediately knew something was wrong. Rushing over she saw the inkblot-like circle of blood that had leaked from the dead woman's head.

"Andrea? Oh my God! No. No." she said in a low tone that could only be heard by somebody in the same room; not a scream or a shriek as they always seemed to do on the telly or in books.

She bent down and was about to touch Andrea's corpse when she noticed the legs protruding from the bedroom door. She got up and moved to the white body.

"Jesus Christ," she exclaimed in the same hushed tone as she saw the state of the dead body and brought her hands to her mouth to stop throwing up.

Lydia ran to the kitchen and drank a cup of water as she got herself together. She washed and then dried the glass, lit a cigarette and took a deep pull before walking into the bedroom where she opened a cupboard and removed some photos from an album.

Lydia was about to leave the bedroom, when she thought again. She opened the wardrobe, selected a large expensive holdall and packed it with some of the designer clothes and a few other items she felt Andrea would not have objected to her taking.

Lydia took a last look around. She felt certain she had wiped down the flat thoroughly enough not to leave a single fingerprint. Although she had packed the holdall with clothes, Andrea's laptop and both the girls' mobile phones, she had deliberately left their purses untouched. She was no thief; everything she had taken would not be missed and would only have been retained by the police. Surely it was better for a friend to make use of them?

Lydia walked to the bus stop where she waited nervously in the late night until a red bus appeared. She hopped on, went upstairs and sat alone deep in thought. After a ten-minute ride, Lydia got off the bus, walked down a side street and into a phone box. She dialled 999.

"Go to flat 28 Napier Court, Blackheath."

"Can you give ...." the Police operator started.

Quickly hanging up the phone, she wiped it with the sleeve of her jacket and hurried out of the booth.

Declan rang the bell and waited expectantly. He peered through the letterbox to see that the bed-sit was in darkness.

"Come on Marcus open up. I know you're in there," Declan shouted.

He rang the bell again, but there was still no answer. He scribbled a note, pushed it through the letterbox and walked away shaking his head.

Marcus waited until Declan's footsteps receded, then bent down, picked up the note, which he read before crumpling it up and tossing it away. He went back inside, switched on the TV and watched a news programme. There had still been no announcement either on the TV or in the papers. Perhaps the woman he had seen at Andrea's window had not wanted to get involved. Perhaps she had not reported it.

When the news was over, he walked to the window and stood staring at Andrea's flat. He stayed there until the night closed in before sitting down to watch the late news bulletin.

Mid morning saw Marcus placing the cereal bowl in the sink that was already full of dirty dishes. He walked to the window and stared as a police car pulled up outside Andrea's block. Two uniformed officers got out and entered the building. After some time an ambulance pulled up behind the police car and the crew disappeared inside Napier Court.

Marcus watched as more cars arrived before he left the window and turned on the TV. He chewed nervously on his lips. The wheels were now in motion, surely it was now only a matter of time before they came to question or arrest him.

Claudia St Clair sat behind her desk dealing with the mundane paperwork that had built up during her fortnight's leave. Her jacket hung on a wooden hanger behind her office door as she worked in her shirtsleeves. She was interrupted by a knock on the door as a uniformed Sergeant stuck his head around the door.

"The Superintendent wants you in his office Inspector," the Sergeant announced.

"Thanks Colin, I'm on my way."

She stood up, smoothed the new purple skirt she had got from Principles, took the matching jacket from the hanger, and walked along the corridor to an open office where a uniformed Superintendent looked up from the file he was reading and beckoned her inside. He offered her a chair, closed the file and took off his glasses.

"Welcome back Claudia. Trust you had a good leave."

"Yes thanks sir," Claudia replied, closing the door and taking a seat.

"I take it you've heard about the double murder in Blackheath."

"Yes sir."

"Good. I want you in charge."

"Right sir."

The phone in front of him rang.

"I've assigned DS Morgan and DC Elford to work with you," Superintendent Middleton said, pushing the file across his desk before dismissing DI St Clair with a wave and picking up the phone.

Claudia walked back down the corridor to another open office where three plain-clothes officers were talking.

"Taff, my office please."

The balding, ginger haired Welshman stroked his moustache and hoisted his tall heavily built frame from the chair. Now aged fifty-four and with over twenty years service, he had accepted the fact that he had reached as far as he would in the force. He realised he was good at giving and taking orders, but would never be the one in overall command. The years served as a Chief Petty Officer in the Navy had taught him that a good leader was generally accompanied by a good second-in-command, and he was satisfied that both his superiors and his subordinates alike recognised his qualities.

He had worked with DI St Clair before and they had an easy, friendly relationship due to the fact that they both respected each other.

Taking the few paces down the buff-tiled corridor, scented with disinfectant, he remembered their first run-ins: the sturdy black woman, hell-bent on her rise through the ranks, frequently prickly, always watchful for a slur on her sex or ethnic origin, anticipating disrespect.

In those days she had based her style with him on her own grandmother's, he recalled. She'd admitted it later. His worst offence had been a trivial slip in his newly mastered Politically Correct vocabulary; referring to a local 'working girl' as a 'Tom'. A local working girl that had happened to be black.

He had done the referring in a context where her blackness had been relevant ("of the essence", had been Claudia's way of putting it), owing to the fact that her clientele was deeply involved at a bottom-feeding level with clubs and drugs, and spoke a street language that he hadn't been able to penetrate. Sometimes in texts via their mobile phones, this had been even worse.

Knowing Melishia fairly well from buying her the odd cup of coffee, normally at the Turkish cafe across the road when she had information for sale, and warning her off the street corners when Vice were on a mission to clean up the streets; Taff had turned to her for enlightenment.

Claudia had spotted them having a lesson in the cafe, had seen Taff slipping the girl a twenty-pound note. She'd interrupted and Melishia had stormed off in a mighty huff. Taff was accused of taking advantage.

"First honest hour's work she's done in three years, and I'm taking advantage? Says on her cards, she gives 'special tuition, home or hotel visits possible'. Seen them all over, in the phone boxes, see," he explained, greatly amused. Claudia was new to the station.

He'd leant forward earnestly over the empty cups. "I don't think you understand, love. Being a 'Tom', she knows a bit about our

48

suspects, even if its second hand from the runners and such; sometimes a bit higher up. She's a bit of a looker and she understands the language these Afro and Rasta lot use in their rapping and all that. Need some help with it, I do, and the Met hasn't offered any training for it, see? They don't give a rat's ringbolt about a poor old Welshman lost in the big city. It's not like Barry Island where I come from, see," he finished, clearly grossly exaggerating a normally hardly noticeable Welsh accent.

Briefly, he had wondered if Claudia was actually going to have a stroke. Then she had started to laugh, great gusts and bellows of it. Since then, the two had got on fairly well. Both from persecuted races, they agreed.

"Right Inspector," he answered.

The pair walked to her office. She removed her jacket and replaced it on the hanger. "Have a seat," she said, moving behind her desk and opening the file.

"What have we got?"

"Not a lot. Two women both struck over the head repeatedly. We've got the murder *weapon*; a smashed champagne bottle was left behind. Forensic hasn't turned up anything much so far; no prints. They are still testing for DNA and any fibres on the bodies."

"Have we got *anything* to start on?"

"We've got the names of both victims. DC Elford's checking them out. We need to get statements from the neighbours. I can't believe someone didn't hear something."

"Fine. I'll leave it up to you to organise bods to go knocking on doors."

"Okay."

"Give me a while to read this and get up to speed, then we can get this show on the road."

Marcus entered the café opposite the police station.

"What can I get you?" the Turkish assistant asked.

"Black coffee please."

"Anything else?"

"No thanks."

The assistant made the coffee, took Marcus' money and returned to his duties. Marcus walked to a table beside the window and fixed his eyes on the police station opposite, watching as civilians and people in uniforms entered and exited the doors. The urge to cross the road and get it over with gnawed away.

It was all he could think about. What had possessed him? How had he thought he would get away with it? It was still not too late. All he had to do was cross the road, open the door and lay down his burden. No more guilt! He sighed wearily and took a mouthful of the strong black coffee.

Dusty light filtered into DC Stephanie Elford's soft, honey blonde coiled-up hair through the grubby slatted blind of the Police Station's open plan CID room, where she sat feeding data into field boxes on her computer screen while ending a one-handed telephone conversation. She hadn't lingered over long over her styling: a big tortoiseshell comb held the whole gorgeous mass of waves aloft.

Stephanie had drawn a whole handful of lucky long straws at birth. Looks and brains. A fairly good figure ("she's got a good pair on her," were words Stephanie had overheard on many occasions), grey eyes, dark brows, small classical features. She had a caring disposition, with 'a sense of humour deficit rivalling the Watford Gap', her former DS had complained.

She was known to be religious, but her views and feelings – though strong - were hard to read. You could often tell that Stephanie would disapprove of something, only it was against her principles to disapprove.

Certainly it was known that her boyfriend Tim worked in television and was a committed Buddhist; and Stephanie was also *very involved*. But you could never quite tell whether one of her attitudes was a Buddhist thing, or just personal, or the way Stephanie happened to be reacting at that moment or simply because it was the wrong time of the month.

Stephanie chanted occasionally at work, but always inconveniently, to recharge her batteries. She favoured health foods, notwithstanding the lentils and what the same former DS reprehensibly dubbed "Pikey tea" (he had been threatened with disciplinary procedure for coming out with that in the canteen).

Stephanie knew how to flirt. This talent would be well wasted on Claudia, and as she put down the phone, the twenty-five-year-old decided to keep her report simple. She hadn't come up with much yet on the Napier Court killings, and there was little point in flamming it up. There was no way she was going to mess up the chance of shining on this her first murder case.

"I've got the run down on the victims," she announced, as she entered Claudia's office.

"Let's hear it."

Stephanie started reading from her notepad. "The black woman was Andrea Bailey. She was twenty-five years old. She came to London from Devon about six years ago. Her mother was a single parent who died from cancer. Her grandfather's alive. The locals went round to see him. He says he hadn't heard from her since her mother died." Stephanie, never afraid to comment added, "Which is tragic in itself."

"No really? What about her father?"

"Apparently she never knew him. She came to London to try and find him."

"Did she?"

"Well she's been living in London for six years," Stephanie patiently hinted. "She wasn't visiting."

"*Find* him?" Claudia all but howled.

Where another Detective Constable would have shrugged, DC Elford went extra still. "I don't know yet," she said carefully. "We do know she got herself a job in a department store, but only stayed for six months. After that, she worked as a receptionist in a hotel in Earl's Court. She wasn't there long either; she left after a year. Since then nothing; she wasn't signing on though."

"Why did she leave the jobs? Anything there?"

Stephanie shook her head. "She wasn't sacked from the store; she worked out her notice. Can't say about the hotel, it's been sold twice since she was there."

"Has she got any previous?"

"Nothing so far. I'll keep working on it."

Claudia St Clair drew in her finely chiselled nostrils and breathed out through them, slowly, in pure exasperation.

Stephanie briefly considered explaining to her boss how chanting would help Claudia to weather the stresses of this investigation, but the moment passed.

"She's not working, she's not signing on and she hasn't got any previous. Terrific! Right, let's find out where she's been living for the last six years. Get someone to go through her bills and bank account. "

"The bad news guv is that Andrea paid six months rent for Napier Court in cash. She dropped in monthly to the letting agency to pay the bills for electricity and services - again in cash. All the staff could tell us was to confirm that it was her. We've seemed to hit a brick wall," said Stephanie.

"Can I get some good news? How long had she lived in Napier Court? She must have given her previous address to the letting agency," asked a deflated Claudia.

"She'd been there for just over three months and gave an address in Devon as her last address."

"She drove, so let's check for parking tickets. Someone must know her," Claudia paused for a moment. "What about the other one?"

Stephanie pulled out another sheet. "Michelle Warner, twenty-two-years-old; she was working as a table dancer at a club in the West End. She lived in a bed-sit in Wandsworth."

Claudia interrupted, "I want you to go and look round it later, see what you can turn up."

Stephanie nodded. "Will do. I've spoken to her parents. They live in Kent - Orpington. She visited them regularly, at least once a month. They didn't know where she worked – thought she was in a West End show, which I suppose she was in a way. She obviously didn't want them to know what she did and kept it from them."

"Did they know Andrea?"

"Hadn't a clue who she was."

"Why am I not surprised?"

"They couldn't think of anyone who would harm her. I'll try and get a list of mates, ex-boyfriends and people she may have worked with."

"Ok. We also need to check if she made any calls on the night of the murder. Could give us a lead."

"The landline wasn't connected and there's no mention of mobile phones on the property sheets," Stephanie informed her boss.

"Come on everybody has a mobile these days," an infuriated Claudia said.

"Right, I'll get on that too," said Stephanie, wondering how much of the boring mundane tasks she was going to be called upon to do during this case. Okay so she was the least experienced, but that did not mean that she was going to be just a lackey. As soon as they finished this chat, she would go and chant.

Stephanie wanted to go home. This had already been a long day and she had been pencilled in to help with a special session for children at her Buddhist group.

She enjoyed working with young children who liked her intensity, which mirrored their own normal obsessive behaviour. Young adolescents latched on to Stephanie only now and again. Her insistence in seeing only the good in everyone bothered them – was she a phoney or just mental? When they discovered that she was a detective, deep suspicion set in.

DS Morgan opened the door. "Copies of the Medical Report," he said waving the file and handing them across to Claudia who read them then passed them across to DC Elford.

"Cause of death - bloody obvious," Stephanie said reading aloud.

"A case of 'brut' force," Taff stated with a wry smile.

"Time of death...." Stephanie looked up, "that means it wasn't reported for two days."

"Any news on the caller Taff?"

"Nothing. All we know is that the call was made by a woman from a phone box in Lewisham."

"How about CCTV pictures?"

"None. She called from a side street with no cameras. No chance."

Stephanie looked up from the report again. "It says here no semen was present in either women, but both had evidence of recent sexual activity."

Taff shot her an incredulous look, "How old are you? I thought your generation always preached safe sex! Condoms would explain no semen. Plus I would hope if there had been unprotected sex, then there would have been some morning after pills in the place, wouldn't you?"

"Just thinking aloud. Could it have been a casual pick up who went crazy then?"

"Could be. What I'd like to know is how and where did they meet? That might give us a start. So far all we've got is a mystery woman and a stripper." Claudia stated. "What were they doing at Andrea's flat?"

"Well there's no sign of a break-in, so presumably whoever did this must have been known to them; or at least one of them," Stephanie chipped in.

"Unless as you said it was a casual pick up."

"Not stating the bleeding obvious, but we've got to find out where they were before they got killed," Taff said.

"Shame Napier Court didn't have entry cameras," Stephanie remarked.

Darren Turner clambered awkwardly from the blue Ford Transit, picked up the canvas bag that contained his brushes and equipment, then slammed the passenger door shut.

"See you at seven tomorrow," his uncle Pete shouted as he slammed the van into gear and sped off, cutting up the car behind him whose driver sounded his horn angrily.

Darren walked up the path and neared the door; he could hear the frantic scratching behind it. He turned the key in the lock and quickly stuck out a foot to stop the eagerly advancing Staffordshire terrier. "Get off Rooney," he yelled as he shut the front door, fussed the dog then kicked off his paint-splattered boots.

"Me mum."

"Your tea's in the oven," a voice from the living room cried out.

"In a minute, I'm going out later. I'll eat after my bath."

He eased out of his white overalls, dumped them on top of the canvas bag, trotted upstairs and turned on both taps before going into his bedroom. He tugged the sweaty T-shirt over his head and thought of the night ahead, wondering whether he would need any protection. As he climbed out of his dirty jeans, he decided not to build his hopes up, he would let the night take its course and go with the flow. Darren wrapped a towel round his waist and went to the bathroom.

Chapter 7

Marcus entered the *Market Tavern* and immediately felt an atmosphere or buzz in the air. There was a large lunchtime crowd and as he walked to the bar, he contemplated turning around, but fought the urge and waited uncomfortably at the bar until the middle-aged barmaid finished serving a customer then moved across to Marcus. She took a glass from under the counter and started pulling a pint when he gave her his order.

"Heard the news?"

Marcus shook his head.

"They found a couple of bodies in Napier Court. Murdered."

"Really?"

"Yes. It's been in the news, on the telly. The police have been asking questions." She nodded to a group of around twenty men and women seated close to the door, "Now we've got the journalists snooping around."

Marcus shrugged. "Must have missed it. Who were they?"

"Two young girls. One of them has been in here a couple of times, young half-caste girl." The barmaid finished pouring the pint, took his money and deposited it in the till. "Napier Court," she shook her head, "you're not safe anywhere nowadays."

She handed Marcus his change and turned to serve another waiting customer.

Marcus took his pint and sat down alone. At the table beside him, he could hear people talking about the recent murder. He listened into their conversation, surreptitiously scanning people in the pub. He finished his pint quickly before leaving the pub and the staring, accusing eyes.

Marcus walked from the pub, stood opposite Napier Court watching to see who came and left the block when Natasha emerged from Lambton House wearing a brand new tracksuit and trainers. She turned down the volume of the Ipod, removed her earphones and let them rest between her shoulders.

"Hi Marcus. How are you?" she asked chirpily.

"Okay."

"What've you been up to?"

"Nothing. Nothing at all," Marcus said guiltily.

"Are you alright?"

"Yes. Just had some bad news that's all."

"What about?"

"Oh a job I went for," he lied.

"I'm sorry," Natasha consoled, reaching her hand to his shoulder.

Marcus recoiled from her kindly gesture. "It's not your fault is it?"

"What are you doing this weekend?" she asked ignoring his lack of warmth.

"I don't know."

"Are you going out anywhere?"

"No."

"Good. I'll try and drop in if you don't mind."

"It's up to you."

"Okay. I've got to rush. Bye," she smiled.

"See you."

Claudia St Clair shut the door and sat down with her two colleagues. "Taff, I want you and Stephanie to go down to Cornwall and speak to the grandfather, see what he has to say. It could be someone from her life down there."

"Okay," said the Welshman.

"And I want you to find out as much as you can about her father."

"Right."

"I'll go and see the people in Orpington."

"Lucky you," Stephanie said.

Marcus lay in bed with the curtains drawn although it was only mid morning. He watched a news report on the TV giving details of the murder. A black policewoman who was introduced as DI St Clair, appeared on screen with a reporter.

"Someone knows who did this. If you have anything you believe will help us catch this person, please contact us. I assure you your call will be treated in the strictest confidence," the black policewoman spoke into the camera.

"Thank you Inspector," the reporter said, ending the report.

The knocking of the letter box did not surprise Marcus. He switched off the TV, went to the front door and peered through the spy hole before opening the door. He had seen the team of officers walking down the street from his window and had been waiting for them to come knocking on his door. He took a deep breath before opening the door.

"Hello sir. We're conducting enquiries into an incident that occurred in Napier Court last weekend. Do you mind answering a few questions?" the young policeman asked with a warm smile on his face.

"No."

"May we come in sir?"

"Oh, of course."

"Thank you," the second, older policeman said as they moved past Marcus into the stuffy bed-sit. Marcus showed them to the sofa and sat on the bed.

"You've heard about the murder?" the young one asked. It seemed that he was the one in charge.

"Yes."

"Did you know either of the victims?"

"I don't know."

"Have you seen the pictures of them?"

"No I'm sorry, I haven't."

The second officer reached into the manila envelope he was holding, produced copies of photographs of both girls and handed them across to Marcus.

"Did you know them?"

Marcus examined the images. "No I didn't. I think I may have seen one of them in the pub."

"Which one would that be?" the young detective asked.

"Her," Marcus said, pointing to the picture of Andrea.

"When did you last see her?"

"Middle of last week I think. Yes, Wednesday."

"Did you speak to her?"

"No, I was with a friend."

"I see. Have you ever spoken to her before?"

"No."

"That Wednesday, did she act or behave strangely?"

"Not to my knowledge, but I don't know her and didn't take much notice of her."

"I understand. Did you see or hear anything unusual over the weekend?"

"No."

"But you were around?" the second officer chipped in.

"Yes."

"Do you mind telling us what you were doing?" the older one continued, his tone a lot firmer and less friendly than that of his young colleague.

"I was here watching the TV."

"All over the weekend?"

"Most of it yes."

"And you didn't notice anything unusual?" the young one said, now bouncing off his colleague's questions.

"No."

"There was nobody acting peculiarly or any strangers hanging around?" the older one asked.

"Sorry, I never saw anything."

"Well thanks for your time sir. If you think of anything that might be helpful, please don't hesitate to contact us," the younger one said, handing Marcus a card as he got up to leave. His colleague walked to the window and took a cursory look before joining his partner as Marcus showed them out.

Once outside the bed-sit, the young officer turned to his partner. "Not much help."

"Nope. Pity, his flat looks right out onto Napier Court."

"Come on. You can do the talking this time," he said as they walked along to the next flat and knocked on the door.

Natasha put the magazine down as the ridiculously young looking assistant walked towards her.

"Would you like a drink?" the girl asked.

A few minutes later, still astonished at her own daring and extravagance, Natasha cocooned in a charcoal-grey smock, returned her own hazel-eyed solemn gaze in the lozenge-shaped mirror. Joanne the senior stylist deftly twisted up coils of Natasha's soft, ash-brown hair, and clipped them in place with little metal butterflies, the better to snip at the section where work was in progress. In a circle on the floor lay the trimmings.

Joanne was skilful. Once they had established that Natasha wasn't going on any holiday anytime soon, and that she liked running, they had dropped the pretence of small talk and got down to business. Mutual respect was born. Joanne loved transforming heads of hair that were unclogged with 'product' - leave-in conditioners, mousses, gels, dyes – and silky with health. Moreover, she yearned to put in some highlights. She wanted to keep this girl, and have her back for treatment.

"I want to give it a bit of definition," said Joanne. "Hold your head a tiny bit up for me, would you? And I want it to have …. just a little bit of attitude? You know? Just the hint of spikiness around the crown?"

"A touch of *don't mess with me*?" Natasha put in wickedly, reaching carefully for her cup of cooling coffee, so as not to move her head.

Joanne laughed self-assuredly. "I don't think you need conditioner. You've kept it lovely and natural, but if you're running everyday, and washing it, you might like to take some of our 'Jean-Simon Washaday' shampoo home. A bottle lasts ages."

Stephanie Elford got out from the driver's seat of the Ford Focus and walked round to join Taff. They strode across the gravel driveway up to a smart detached house. Taff rang the bell and a distinguished looking elderly white man with thick bi-focal glasses cautiously opened the door.

"Good morning, Mr Bailey?"

"Yes," the man replied, looking over his glasses as he studied the stranger.

"DS Morgan, Metropolitan Police," the Welshman announced producing his warrant card, which the man inspected closely before removing the door chain to allow the two detectives inside.

"Come in officers," he smiled. "One can't be too careful. You don't know who to trust nowadays eh?"

"That's quite alright Mr Bailey. This is DC Elford."

Bailey nodded, but declined Stephanie's outstretched hand, turned and led the way to a neat, well-organised sitting room. "Can I get you something to drink? Tea, coffee or perhaps something cold after your long journey?" he offered.

"A cup of tea would be lovely thanks," Taff replied.

Bailey turned to Stephanie, "and you officer?"

"Tea's fine."

With that he shuffled off, returning a few minutes later with a teapot, cups, saucers, milk and sugar on a trolley. He poured two cups of tea, handed them across to the officers. "Please help yourself to milk and sugar," he said easing himself to the green leather armchair.

Stephanie sat with Taff on a three-piece leather sofa – the counterpart to the armchair from where Bailey now looked at them (or rather at Taff). She declined both milk, sugar, and took a sip of the strong, rich tea. She looked around the room. It was a cold room, full of well-made pieces of furniture, yet totally lacking in character.

A large walnut bookcase occupied an entire wall. On the other walls, hung several pictures; one of a younger Bailey with two women Stephanie presumed were his late wife and daughter. Beside the younger woman, an even more youthful version of Bailey (perhaps his son?) stood with arm draped over the shoulder of the daughter. Another picture showed Bailey proudly in the uniform of an officer in the Army; his wife wearing a thin knee-length white dress and wide brimmed hat. Other pictures in the room showed Bailey in the company of a variety of important looking men.

Stephanie noted that not one picture of Andrea could be seen in the room.

"Now officer?" Bailey said addressing DS Morgan.

Taff gave Stephanie a knowing look, which she returned with a dutiful grimace to indicate that she too had picked up on the man's misogynistic manner. "I gather you know why we're here Mr Bailey?"

"Oh yes. The local constabulary came round."

"We'd just like to ask a few questions that might help us solve this matter."

"I understand. Ask away," Bailey smiled.

"I gather you hadn't seen Andrea for some while," said Taff.

"That's right. She left her mother alone as soon as she reached sixteen."

"When *did* you last see her?"

Bailey removed his glasses, folded them deliberately and placed them on the coffee table. "At my daughter's – *Andrea's* mother's funeral."

Stephanie noticed the difficulty that he had saying Andrea's name.

"Which was when sir?" Taff asked.

"Three years ago Sergeant. She attended the service, but didn't stay for the wake. Said she didn't belong here anymore once her mother had gone. Probably right."

Taff noted the tone. He took a sip of his tea, glanced over to his colleague, and was pleased that she cottoned-on and took up the questioning.

"And you hadn't seen or heard from Andrea since the funeral?" Stephanie asked.

"That's right," Bailey answered dismissively, still addressing Taff as though he had posed the question.

"Had she been in touch before her mother's death?" Stephanie persisted.

"After she left, she would ring her mother every now and then; usually for money."

"Did she ever return to visit?"

"Yes she did. Not often. When she found out her mother had cancer she came down once or twice. She even stayed with her for a week or so."

"So she got on with her mother?"

Bailey made a protracted move for the drinks trolley before answering. "They were very close for a long time."

He paused and poured himself a cup of tea.

Stephanie noticed the pause. "But something happened to change that?"

"'*Kunta Kinte*,'" he said with contempt.

"Pardon?"

"Oh I'm sorry. You're probably too young to understand. '*Roots*'. She wanted to find her sire," Bailey said, smiling smugly.

Taff realised what the man meant and quickly stepped in. "I see. How did her mother feel about that?"

61

"It was something she had been dreading, yet knew was probably going to happen," Bailey answered nonchalantly. He slowly raised the cup from the saucer and drank some of the tea; taking a pause before replacing the cup.

Feeling more at ease now that he was once again talking to a man, Bailey turned his back on the female detective. "You see my daughter just turned up one day and out of the blue announced she is a mother. Just like that. As if that wasn't enough of a shock, she produces her 'little brown baby'."

He coughed at the obviously painful memory.

"I'm not going to lie to you," he continued, managing to keep his composure although he was obviously irate. "Jesus Christ! Thérèse hurt us a great deal. The scandal and gossip we had to face. She really suffered you know; Margaret my poor late wife! It may even have hastened her death. You should have heard what some people in our neighbourhood used to say to my wife's face when the situation became known. Back then we had values and standards we lived by. We tried to discuss it sensibly with her; tried to make Thérèse see that it was best if she had the baby adopted; but she wouldn't hear of it. Very headstrong my daughter."

He finished his tea and placed the cup back on the trolley.

"Anyway as you know she kept the child and struggled to make something of her life. Bloody well wasted her life!"

"Do you know if Andrea found her father?" Stephanie asked even though she could see Taff was not happy with her taking a lead role.

Bailey made no attempt to hide his anger. "I neither know nor care! Whoever the black bastard was, he defiled my daughter, impregnated and then abandoned her; leaving us to bring up his pickaninny! If only she had told us earlier, we could have made arrangements to take care of the problem."

Seeing the shock on the faces of the two officers, he composed himself, smiled and added, "I'm not going to apologise. Mine was a different generation to yours. We weren't afraid to call a spade a spade."

Taff shot Stephanie a glance before picking up the questioning. "Did your daughter tell Andrea who her father was?"

"I would have thought so. When the illness started to get pretty bad, I think she wanted her to know. Thérèse was certain she wouldn't find him and would return to be with her; of course she didn't."

"Did she tell *you* who he was?"

"No Sergeant she didn't."

"Did Andrea have many friends down here? Anyone she might have kept in touch with after she left?" Stephanie asked.

"I'm not really the one to ask. I don't think so. She really didn't fit in. I suppose she needed to be with her own kind."

"Any boyfriends?"

"I really wouldn't know," Bailey smiled sweetly.

"Andrea wasn't working; do you know if she had any means of support?"

"Yes she did. When Thérèse died she left her everything."

"How much would that have been?"

"Well she sold the house and contents. I think the total estate was worth around seventy five thousand pounds after deductions."

Taff thought of trying a new tack. "Did you know Michelle Warner Mr Bailey?"

"No. Why should I?" he answered without hesitation.

"I just wondered. She was also killed with Andrea; but you never met her?"

"No."

Stephanie could not contain herself any longer. "Mr Bailey how did you get on with Andrea?"

Bailey stared at the policewoman contemptuously before responding in an emotionless tone, "I never blamed her."

"But surely she knew how you felt?"

Bailey struggled to contain his anger. "My wife and I always made sure she got presents on her birthday and at Christmas. I never blamed her; it wasn't her fault. She was our first grandchild. She had my blood, I should've been proud, but I wasn't, I just could never love her the way I wanted."

Taff realised he had to get things back in order. "You can think of no one who would have wanted to kill her?"

"No."

"Well I don't think there's anything else. Thank you for your help," the Welshman concluded, sensing that the interview was not going to progress any further.

"When do you think they'll release the body?" Bailey asked.

The two officers looked at each other in disbelief.

"I have to make arrangements to bury her. Her mother would never forgive me; and despite everything, she was my grandchild."

"We'll let you know as soon as possible," Taff said concealing the scorn from his voice.

Taff and Stephanie walked back across the gravel driveway. "And I wonder why Andrea ran away?" Stephanie hissed once in the car.

"I was wondering why she waited so long," Taff said buckling his seatbelt. This was going to be some drive home.

"Wait till the Inspector hears this," Stephanie said slamming the car into gear irately and driving off.

Both officers were more comfortable at Sally Wilkes' house. It was a roomy terraced house, Victorian but pleasingly plain and white; set on the green of a well-kept village one mile out of Tregarth, a small market town that showed symptoms of thriving; with a nearby trading estate and distribution centre mushrooming just off the motorway. The Wilkes' walled garden was beginning to bloom through the sliding patio doors of a study with sofa bed, lightwood workstation and wicker chairs. Bookshelves and files, a small television, computer stuff indicated a room for the family to use as and when needed.

Mrs Sally Wilkes, once Miss Sally Geyer of Styne Oak Junior School, looked at her two unexpected visitors. Twenty years after the scenes of Andrea's unhappy childhood experiences, she had gained a few pounds and her face had acquired lines in telling places, adding character rather than dowdiness to her features.

Being the school holidays, Sally (now a headmistress), was working from home while her teenage offspring roamed the premises. Stephanie and Taff heard the pad of trainer-clad feet, the soft thunk of a fridge door closing, the drone of a microwave ("D Sharp!" thought Taff inconsequentially, identifying the pitch of the microwave with help of a good musical ear and years of choir training in his early adolescence).

He came back to the present with a jolt, as Sally effortlessly raised her well-modulated voice to bellow. "Arabella! Can you bring us three coffees please!"

"You had three cups of coffee at breakfast. All that caffeine's bad for you. I'll bring you some nice Green tea," floated the soprano response.

"That would be lovely," said Stephanie, wistfully.

"She's so bossy," said Sally apologetically.

"Don't bother arguing Mum!" uttered a young baritone. "It's not worth the pain. She won't even let me have some – OWW!! Bella that hurt! Mum! She's beating me up!"

There came sounds of giggling and squeals, howls of mock anguish, and scuffling.

"Shut up, both of you. I've got the police here. You'll get asboed," Sally shouted.

"Nah. Bet they've come about dad and his French horn playing."

"Or his parking."

Once Arabella had redeemed herself by bringing in a tray with both coffee and herbal options in seldom-used pots, plus milk and other accoutrements, all the while smiling radiantly, Sally called the meeting to order.

"I was horrified to hear about poor Andrea Bailey. But, you know what, that wasn't the most surprised I've been in my life. That child has haunted me. We've heard bits and pieces about the family over the years, and some of it's been less than pleasant. My husband had contact with the grandfather professionally, you see."

She looked as if she were going to pull a face of distaste, but stopped just in time.

"I changed schools after I married, and anyway teachers get to hear about stuff, so I got the occasional update about Andrea. For me, the worry really started one time in the playground at Styne Oak – the other children sort of mobbed her. Danced round her singing that Boney M song 'Brown Girl In The Ring'. It was ugly," Sally said then sipped her coffee guiltily.

"I was just rushing out to break it up, when her mother turned up. She'd called in with some project work that the little girl couldn't carry to school herself. Just dragged her off and out of it; I couldn't catch them up. When they reached the gate Andrea heard me shout, and she turned round and gave me such a look, as if she thought I could stop all the bad things in her life. She always struck me after that as a child that bad things were happening to; and it wasn't just being a posh, mixed-race pupil at a rough state school. I knew that was hard on her, and my advice was part of the reason she went on to the convent. Roman Catholic schools do tend to be more racially diverse, you know, especially in the country."

She told a good story; both Stephanie and Taff were hooked.

"No, it was more than that. It was almost as if the kids knew something else about her, and she sort of accepted it was true, so she couldn't be angry and fight back. Almost as if she thought she encouraged it. Poor troubled girl, she deserved her share of happiness, at least now she'll be at peace."

In the silence that followed, Arabella could be clearly heard lecturing her brother about excessive milk drinking.

"Yes, Bella there will be enough left for breakfast tomorrow, and no, *I hadn't* forgotten Mum was holding the Village Book Club here because it's too cold in the Church Hall, and I *insist* you stop nagging," her brother reproached.

Sally rose ponderously from the armchair she had settled comfortably into, "I'll be back in a minute," she said making a helpless gesture with her hands.

"Is this the Vicarage?" Taff demanded of his colleague. "There's one of their wedding photos on the wall over there, and he isn't in a dog collar, the husband, I mean."

Stephanie followed his gaze. Sally had never been pretty. She had been – and still was - attractive. There she was, not so different, in a knee-length ivory satin two-piece, topped by a chic little hat with a hint of veil, bearing freesias. Beside her was a startlingly good-looking man in his early thirties, with small regular features and a satin tie that co-ordinated with Sally's outfit. He was prettier than his wife or daughter, she thought.

Stephanie, whose research had discovered Andreas's teacher and subsequently her married name and address, frowned. "I don't remember any reference to Sally marrying a Reverend anyone," she told her colleague. "Is it significant?"

"Confidentiality issues and professional ethics," grumbled Taff.

Stephanie dropped her voice. "She knows a lot more than she's telling, and she wants us to know that. What do you reckon? Push her, or what?"

"No point in pushing. Let's see what she comes up with on her own. We can always come back if we need to."

At that moment Sally returned, her wiry auburn hair rumpled, as if she had been running her hands through it. She closed the door and settled back in her chair again. Recklessly, like a drunkard downing his first straight scotch of the day, Sally seized her forgotten coffee cup and downed the cold stuff in one swallow.

She restarted without warning, her voice just above a whisper, "Look this is gossip, but the word was that Andrea's mum had a hard time getting access to the money her own mother left her in Trust. They were really broke, she and the child, until the funds came through when Andrea was about ten."

Sally reached for the cup; only realising it was empty when she picked it up. She had them on the edge of their seats now.

"I'm not sure whether it was her pride or plain stubbornness, but Thérèse Bailey would never accept outside help. Even though she had family, it was always just the two of them against the world."

"Thérèse took little jobs in shops even though she was educated and very artistic; well she did go to Art College in London when she was younger. Eventually she found a job with a department store in Plymouth and ended up becoming a Buyer for the company."

She was just about to go on with her account when a deafening crash came from the kitchen, followed quickly by an ear-splitting painful howl.

"Mum, Adam's fallen off the chair and hurt himself," Bella's concerned voice yelled.

Sally Wilkes sprung from the armchair and raced into the kitchen. Her horrified scream brought the two officers running in behind her to be greeted by the sight of her son writhing in agony; his arm bent unnaturally with the bone protruding from his skin.

"Dear Lord Adam, what have you done?" She signalled to her daughter, "Bella, time to put your first aid to use. Sort out a sling for your brother. Come on let's get you to hospital." Sally sobbed, reaching for the hook on the wall that held her car keys.

Thoroughly frustrated by the untimely ending of the conversation with Sally Wilkes, the final visit of the day to Our Lady's Covent School only served to confirm to Taff and Stephanie that Andrea Bailey had been a loner who was uncomfortable in the company of others.

Chapter 8

Marcus turned off the TV, reached into the bedside table drawer and found a picture of a young black boy. He closed his eyes and the images returned.

*He could see Maxine's face as she strutted triumphantly out of the court. The judge (a woman of course) had given her sole custody after the bitch had concocted a string of lies. Accusing **him** of unreasonable behaviour and citing the amount of time that he had spent away from home.*

*She had even used the fact that he had trusted her to look after the family finances by producing bank statements from her account, which showed **she** had been the one to make the mortgage payments. The bitch had cruelly, spitefully wiped him from her life and left him ruined.*

If he were caught, he would never see his son again. The thought sent a shiver down Marcus' spine. He wiped a tear from his eye. One moment of madness, (if you discounted the hours he had spent carefully planning the bungled robbery) was that not too high a price to pay?

Natasha tied the laces on her trainers. She left the flat and once on the pavement outside, began her warm-up stretches, no longer embarrassed or conscious whether others thought she looked ridiculous. This was about her.

The running was going well; so well that she had decided it was now time to step up the distance. She set off at a sensible pace, and in no time settled into a steady rhythm, controlling her breathing to minimise the amount of effort she used. As she ran, Natasha reflected on how happy she was. Totally in control.

That's why she had enjoyed the sport at school. Unlike the team games she had been made to play, where the popular girls passed to each other and could be mercilessly cruel to those less gifted or lesser liked, often reducing them to tears and turning some into timid, nervous wrecks; when you ran you were totally in control. There was no one else to rely on or no one else to blame.

Her mind went back to the school cross-country run when she had surprised both herself and the trendy in-crowd by finishing in the top three. Whilst her performance had grudgingly won their respect, they had still not invited her into their clique (as if she would have wanted that).

All it had taken was that inadvertent push from Marcus and now she was experiencing those feelings all over again. The release from constraints - that was what it was about.

Marcus, now there was a thought. She wondered what would happen between them, if anything. So what if he was thirty-four; a full eleven years her senior; *she* knew that what she liked about him was his seeming unawareness of his good looks and his kind, gentle, understanding manner.

But was there a dark side to him? She had noticed the anger when he talked about his ex-wife.

Natasha stepped up her pace as a punishment for the thought. How did she expect someone whose wife had been unfaithful to act? The memory of her mother surfaced and spurred her on.

Claudia turned to her Sergeant. "Right Taff, did we turn up anything in the interviews with the neighbours?"

"Nothing much. No one seems to have known her. She kept herself to herself."

"She'd only moved in a couple of months ago, it's hardly surprising," Stephanie chipped in.

"There's a few worth seeing again. A couple of them said they noticed people hanging about and there's one bloke who lives opposite, he was in all weekend. If we jogged his memory, maybe he might remember something useful."

"Okay. Taff, you and I will go and see them. Michelle's parents were of no use. She left home at nineteen and she never brought any boyfriends back – absolutely nothing," Claudia said.

"Well Andrea's grandfather wasn't much better. He's a bigot, a real racist."

Taff shot the young detective a disapproving glance. He was going to have to have a word with her later about tact.

"Sorry I didn't go down there with you; that would have pleased him," Claudia smiled.

"She definitely didn't confide in him. She had very few friends, certainly none that she kept in touch with, and no boyfriends," said Stephanie.

"What she didn't have any social life at all?"

"If you'd met her grandfather you'd understand."

"But we did get one good piece of news," Taff announced.

"Which was?" Claudia asked.

"She had money. Her mother left her seventy five thousand pounds."

"Wow!" Claudia exclaimed. "Well that explains how she could afford her lifestyle."

"So what next?" Taff asked.

"Stephanie, I want you to go to the club where Michelle worked and see what you come up with. Taff and I will go and see these neighbours."

Darren Turner noted the gang of about twelve or so youths that were hanging around outside the off-licence. Although they all seemed a lot younger than his twenty years, he knew better than to attract their attention and was careful not to look at them in any way that might be interpreted as hostile.

It was well known that in this part of London, 'crews' or 'posses' were not averse to demonstrating their dislike for strangers in physical ways. He was now regretting telling her that he would come over to her place. Darren sighed, as soon as he got out of the area the better.

Stephanie Elford knelt down in front of the Gohonzon - an ornate scroll on which was inscribed Chinese and Sanskrit characters contained in its box (or butsudan). She lit a candle closed her eyes, began chanting 'Nam-myoho-renge-kyo' and went into her buddha state.

Stephanie had first been introduced to Buddhism purely by chance (or had it been destiny) whilst studying at Oxford. It had all started with the finding of an unattended copy of Herman Hesse's

Siddhartha in the Lower Common Room of St Catherine's on a particularly boring night when she had been feeling really low.

Reading that book had led her to a speculative meeting, then to attending several meetings at the temple in Oxford, and eventually visiting the SGI Temple at Taplow Court to receive her Gohonzon. She had now been chanting for over five years.

She chanted for two hours to atone for the time she had missed as a result of the demands made during the investigation; struggling hard at first to purge the memory of the loathsome Bailey and the Wilkes welcoming household.

Darren rang the bell and waited. When the door finally opened, he was greeted with a kiss and hurriedly yanked inside. "We've got the place to ourselves, Mum's working late tonight," the girl smiled.

Marcus as usual, was sitting at his vantage point beside the window looking down, when the blue Ford pulled up outside Napier Court. A tall ginger haired man accompanied by a smartly dressed black woman climbed out of the car and approached the building. From their resolute, authoritative demeanour, he knew straight away that they were police officers. He continued watching as they disappeared inside.

DI St Clair and DS Morgan sat beside each other on the floral sofa opposite Harriet Fawcett, an elderly white woman with a head of thinning white hair, a thin birdlike nose and thin lips. A string of pearls hung around her neck and a small brooch was pinned to her lilac cashmere cardigan. Her tiny frame seemed lost in the matching armchair. A pair of Yorkshire Terriers yapped at their feet, impervious of the annoyance they were causing the pair of detectives.

"I gather you spoke to Andrea, Ms Fawcett," said Claudia.

"Yes I did," the old girl smiled, relishing the attention she seldom received nowadays.

"What did you talk about?"

"Oh nothing in particular. You see I passed her on the day she moved in. She had all these boxes to get up in the lift. I had the girls with me," she said pointing to the dogs. "We just said hello."

Although she looked delicate, it was clear that Harriet Fawcett was in full control of her faculties. Her clipped accent and precise pronunciation made Taff wonder whether the old girl had been plucked from the pages of an Agatha Christie novel.

"And after that?" asked Claudia, trying to ignore the doggy smells that rose from the carpets, seeped through the walls and fell from the ceilings. Slightly miffed that Taff was focussed on gaining the affection of the dogs, patting each in turn, as they ran here and there, in between the furniture occasionally brushing her legs; she turned back to the old lady.

"Again it was just in passing. I always walk the girls before bed. On occasions, we saw each other. She always said hello." The old lady shook her head. "She seemed a nice girl. Who would do such a terrible thing?"

"Did she have many visitors?"

"No, not to my knowledge; I was pleased she wasn't a nuisance. You see the couple who had the flat before were good friends of mine. They retired to Dorset. I was glad the flat had gone to someone decent if you know what I mean," she smiled sweetly.

"So you never saw her with anyone?" Taff asked, totally unaware of how irritating Claudia found his petting of the dogs.

"I do believe I saw her with her father."

"You *met* her father?" Claudia remarked.

"I didn't actually *meet* him. I only saw them together twice. The first time was a few days after she moved in. I suppose he was helping her get the place sorted out. The other time I saw them getting into the lift together."

"Did you get a good look at him?"

"Not really. As I said, I only briefly saw them in passing and my eyesight's not what it used to be."

"Do you think you could try and describe him?"

Ms Fawcett shook her head. "I really don't think so. He was very well dressed though. Wore a very nice suit and had well-polished shoes – that I know. My father always used to say that if a man looked after his shoes then you could be sure he was respectable."

"Was he tall or short?"

"I'm awfully sorry but I really couldn't say."

"Was he dark skinned or light skinned?"

"Oh he wasn't tanned. He had pale skin."

"He was white?" a shocked Taff asked.

"Oh yes! Quite definitely white."

After a further ten minutes, the two detectives realised there was very little else of interest to be gained from the spinster, so Claudia and Taff said thank you to the old girl, left the airless flat, and started walking down the stairs.

"So who was the man?"

"Well he definitely wasn't her father!" Claudia said to her Sergeant.

As they passed an empty flat that was wide open, Claudia noticed the decorators.

"I didn't see any statements from painters or decorators. Did anybody speak to them?"

Taff shrugged his shoulders and followed Claudia as she walked into the flat where a radio was playing loud dance music as the two painters went about their work. Claudia tapped the nearest one on the shoulder as Taff turned down the volume on the radio to the annoyance of the decorator.

"Excuse me, how long have you been working in this flat?" Claudia asked.

The young painter looked her up and down disdainfully before answering "Two weeks. Why?"

She ignored his question, "Were you here all of last week?"

"Yeah."

"Were you working over the weekend?"

"Only the Saturday."

"You know there was a murder in one of the flats?"

"Yeah, that one upstairs."

"Did you see anything unusual at all?"

"Nah."

"Nobody hanging about?"

"Nah."

"Did you see any of the girls on Friday?"

"Saw the black girl go out before we packed up about six o'clock. Are you reporters?"

"She never came back before you left?"

"Dunno. So are you reporters or what?"

Taff flashed his warrant card. "I'd appreciate it if you called in to the station and made a statement."

"What for?" the young lad asked unappreciatively.

"It'll help us eliminate you from our enquiries," Taff added without expression.

"Shit," Marcus said sotto voce, as he looked through the spy hole to see Declan ringing the bell.

"I know you're in there Marcus. I saw the light from the street. I'm not leaving till you open up."

Marcus steeled himself before opening the door and reluctantly allowing his friend inside. Declan turned on the light.

"Fucking hell man," he said, shaking his head and gesturing to the mess

"I know," Marcus muttered apologetically.

"I don't live here mate."

"Sorry, I've been ill."

Declan looked his friend up and down. "Yes, you look like shit. Have you just got up?" the Irishman asked in amazement, which served to let Marcus realise he was still in the same boxers and T-shirt he had been wearing for the past two days.

"Come on, get cleaned up and we'll go for a pint."

"I can't. I haven't any money."

"I'll give you the fucking money. You need to get out."

"I don't really feel up to it."

"Christ Marcus just look at yourself! How long are you going to keep this up? You can't cut yourself off from the real world. Stop feeling sorry for yourself. She's left you, forget her and get on with your life. You used to be a real good laugh."

"Yes, when I was a human being." Marcus replied indifferently.

"Just get yourself together. You've managed to alienate all your other friends," Declan said and tossed Marcus a towel as he started losing his patience. "Get a shower and put some clothes on. I'll clean up this fucking mess."

Taff Morgan sat in his armchair with a bottle of Glenfiddich beside him on the aged coffee table. He broke the seal, poured some into a whisky tumbler, then took a gulp and savoured the woody Malt.

The meeting with Andrea's father had served as reminder of his situation. Here he was alone in his small flat, with no prospects of a relationship on the horizon and the possibility of a lonely retirement all too real. He took another swallow then picked up the phone and dialled the number written in his battered address book.

"Hello?" a well-spoken young, female voice answered.

"Hello Serena."

"Dad!"

"Ah. You still recognise my voice," Taff ribbed, fuelled by the warmth of the whisky.

"Ha-ha. What's the matter? Are you alright?"

"I'm fine. How are you?"

"I'm okay."

"And Laura?"

"A pain as always. She's not here, she's gone out." There was a brief pause. "Are you sure everything's alright?"

"Yes, really. How's college?"

"Stressful. I reckon I'll get a 2/1."

"Is that good?"

"It's a first dad. I'll more than settle for it."

Taff took a large swig before cautiously asking, "How's your mother?"

"She's fine. Look dad what's up?"

"Nothing. It's just a case I'm working on. Made me realise how lucky I am."

"About time."

"When do you go back?"

"Next week."

"Any chance of the three of us meeting up before you go?"

"Sure. I'll have to see when Laura can make it."

"Alright. I'll ring you tomorrow."

"Okay."

"Till tomorrow then."

"Yes don't forget, even if you're working. Okay?"

"I promise."

"And dad."

"What?"

"It's great to hear from you. I love you."

"I love you too. I'm sorry if I don't say it enough."

"I'll forgive you. Just don't forget to phone okay!"

"I won't."

"Look mum's calling me. I've got to go. Speak to you tomorrow."

"Bye darling," Taff said to the dial tone and knocked back the remnants of the glass.

The *Market Tavern* was full of young people getting smashed before going on to the various nightclubs in Lewisham and Catford, or for those keen clubbers ready to make the long journey – Shoreditch and the West End. The deafeningly loud R'n'B music playing in the background had attracted an assorted mixture of black and white, male and female.

"Remember Denise from the office?" Declan shouted above the noise.

"Yes, quiet blonde from up North."

"That's her. You'll never guess what?"

"Well tell me then."

"They caught her giving Simon a blowjob."

"Honest?" Marcus asked dispassionately.

"On my life. Lucky bastard," Declan laughed and finished his pint. "I'll get another round in, might even put a smile on your miserable face."

Declan stood up and made his way to the bar. Marcus looked around the pub with disinterest, wishing that he were still at home in his bed-sit. His attention turned back to Declan who was chatting to two young women. Marcus watched as the Irishman bought the two women a drink and all three started walking towards his table.

"Sharon, Karen; meet Marcus," Declan said, introducing the women after handing Marcus a fresh pint.

"Hi," the two girls said in unison.

"Hello," Marcus replied without much enthusiasm.

"Sharon and Karen are nurses."

Karen smiled at Marcus approvingly; here was a black man with potential. Confident that she looked good for her twenty-seven years, she was wearing her favourite pulling outfit which consisted of a pair of figure hugging jeans and a cropped top that left her flat stomach bare, allowing a partial sight of the tattoo she had had done in Aya Napa. Everyone could see the one that adorned her lower back, however if they managed to fully expose the frontal tattoo; then things had obviously gone more than well.

"Right."

"Marcus and I are in insurance, aren't we mate?"

"Used to be, when I was a human being," Marcus said indifferently.

The girls exchanged a quick dubious glance.

Realising that Marcus was not helping their chances of pulling; Declan quickly stepped in. "So what kind of music are you into ladies?"

"Garage," Sharon giggled.

"I like R'n'B and dancehall. What about you Marcus?" Karen asked, running her fingers teasingly through her shoulder length bottle blonde hair as she mentally undressed him.

"Whatever. I don't really mind."

Karen rolled her eyes to Sharon who turned to Declan. "Look we're going to *Paradox*. Are you coming?"

"Of course we are, aren't we mate?"

Marcus shook his head. "I'm sorry, I feel a bit iffy. You go ahead. I'll be alright. I think I'll have an early night."

Declan looked at his friend in disbelief. "Don't be a killjoy man. Come on it'll be a laugh."

"Honestly Declan I don't feel up to it."

Declan picked up his pint and swiftly downed it. He shot Marcus a dirty look before getting up. "Come on girls let's go."

Marcus watched as the trio left, then finished his pint and walked out of the pub into the night. Without thinking, he walked to the police station and stood opposite watching the officers come and go for half an hour before turning back and returning to his block.

Natasha could hear Wendy and her father laughing in the living room. She knew that Wendy had started on the wine earlier in the afternoon; next, they would be opening the vodka. In a few hours, they would be pissed, and if not arguing with each other, would probably start on her. A night of torment and confrontation was not a prospect that Natasha relished. She looked out of the window and saw Marcus heading towards the block. She checked her hair in the mirror, picked up the plastic bag and headed out of the flat.

Marcus plodded up the stairs and headed to his door. He had just inserted the key when Natasha emerged from her flat carrying a plastic bag.

"Are you going out tonight?"

"No."

He looked up and noticed something unfamiliar about his neighbour. "Have you done something with your hair?" he asked.

Natasha blushed and instinctively raised a hand to her head. "I had it cut and re-styled."

"It looks nice. Really suits you."

"Thanks." She smiled and held up the bag that contained some cans of beer, "Friday night and nowhere to go. Do you mind?"

"No, come in."

He opened the door and they went inside. Natasha sat down on the sofa, opened the bag, passed Marcus a can and took one for herself. "Did you hear about the murder?" she asked as she popped the can open.

"Yes."

"The police came round asking us questions."

"Me too."

Natasha kicked off her shoes and made herself more comfortable. "Do you mind if I wrap one up?"

"What?"

"Wrap a spliff?" she explained, holding up a block of dope.

"Go ahead. I never took you for a smoker."

"Started at Uni, my roommate smokes and suggested I try it, plus it's been a shitty day." She produced a packet of King-sized Rizla's and broke a cigarette. "I couldn't believe it when I saw who it was. I almost died when they showed me her picture. I told the police that we saw her in the pub."

"Did you? What did they say?" Marcus said feigning indifference.

"Nothing much. Just asked me if I knew them and whether they were acting oddly that night," she said, concentrating on the spliff that she had almost finished rolling.

"Yes that's what they asked me."

Natasha lit the spliff and took a drag. "It's a bit scary to think it happened so close."

Marcus sipped from his can. "Hmm."

Natasha blew out a thick cloud of smoke. "I wonder who would do such a thing?"

"Who knows?"

She looked at Marcus in amazement. "Aren't you curious?"

"Not really."

Natasha took another drag, stared at him before passing across the spliff. "That's a bit cold isn't it?"

Marcus accepted the spliff. "Why? It's none of my business."

"Yes, but you must be a bit curious?"

"Curious yes. That's all. Come on, a few days ago you thought she was a whore or a drug dealer."

Natasha almost choked on her beer. "That's not fair. I only said she *could* be, and *you* were the one that started it all off."

"What if you were right though? What if she was involved in something dodgy that went wrong?"

"Christ that's scary."

Marcus took a swig from his can and passed the spliff back. "Who knows what she was up to?" Without missing a beat he added, "Did you tell the police what you thought she was?"

"No. Why should I? I only said she *could* have been into those things."

"What if she was though? What if she deserved what she got?"

Natasha raised her eyebrows. "I can't believe you said that. Nobody deserves that."

"I didn't say she did; I said *what* if she did."

"That's the same thing."

"I don't think so."

Natasha passed the spliff to Marcus and started building another. "I hope they catch whoever did it."

"Do you think they will?"

Natasha shrugged her shoulders. "Who knows?"

Marcus closed his eyes as he emptied the can feeling the effect of the spliff. "I used to dream of killing my ex you know."

She looked into his eyes. "You didn't really mean it."

"I did. I think I would've killed her if I could've got away with it," Marcus said as his thoughts went back to *that* night; recalling the moment when the bottle had smashed into the woman's head. It was as if he had been hitting Maxine.

"That's just the hurt talking," Natasha said as she leant over and kissed him, testing the water. "You're better off without her." She kissed him again, longer, more confidently. "Let it go. I'll look after you."

She made to kiss him again, but this time Marcus pulled away as he snapped back to the present.

"What's the matter?"

"I'm sorry I can't."

"Why, what's wrong?"

"I just can't. It's not you. I really like you; I'm just not ready yet."

She kissed him again, a brief friendly kiss, smiling, relieved that he hadn't flatly rejected her. "I understand, and I can wait. Do you want another can?" she said reaching into the bag and diffusing the situation.

Marcus smiled back at her and accepted the can. "What are you going to do with your degree?"

She took a long pull on the spliff. "I want to go into something useful – maybe fertility or cloning."

"Serious?"

"Yes. It's really fascinating."

"Fucking scary if you ask me."

"Come on. Think how many people's lives can be changed thanks to fertility treatment."

She passed over the spliff.

Marcus shook his head. "I think of it more like Frankenstein. Man trying to play God."

Natasha smiled stupidly. The spliffs were really kicking in now. If only he knew how horny she felt. "Do you believe in God?" she asked.

"After being forced to attend Sunday school and church for so long, I would say not *God*, but my own god."

Natasha's hand wobbled as she reached down for a fresh can. "Which means?"

"Morals, ethics and personal beliefs."

Natasha giggled. "That makes sense," she said sarcastically. "Whose morals and ethics?

"Society's," Marcus managed to say before bursting out in laughter.

"Society is forever changing. A few hundred years ago they burned witches, a hundred years ago women couldn't vote, thirty years ago your own people were treated as second class citizens. Society is about what is acceptable now. I think that in the future it'll be nothing to use these methods."

Marcus raised his hand in surrender. "I think we should have this deep conversation some other time. I really like you – fucked up as your ideas may be."

Natasha smiled and blew him a kiss. "Har-de-har. Someone's stoned."

"Not me," he said laughing.

Natasha started laughing too. "Not much."

"Ok I'm wrecked," Marcus confessed as he teetered to the music system and looked through his collection of music CDs. He picked up Parliament's *Dr Funkenstein*, and blew off the dust. It had been a long time since he had played any music. "Listen to this."

He collapsed into the sofa beside Natasha and the pair giggled away together as the song played.

Chapter 9

Stephanie Elford approached the burly doorman fully aware that he had clocked her as a police officer. Nevertheless, he still asked to see her warrant card before he stepped aside to let her inside.

Stephanie was quietly surprised at the sight that greeted her. The club was smart and well decorated - definitely not a dive. It was softly lit with a Roman theme throughout as suggested by its name – *Tiberius* - with waitresses clad in purple toga styled dresses; not that the girls plying their wares could be classed as 'Vestal Virgins', Stephanie thought. Already several clients were inside, welcoming the attention being paid to them. Two girls were pole dancing while another two were lap dancing in front of well-dressed men.

She walked up to the bar where another two girls sat, picked up a drinks list and took note of the expensive prices. The barman reluctantly moved towards her. Stephanie knew he was not going to be helpful.

"What can I get you?"

"Did you know a girl called Michelle Warner?" she asked politely.

"I only serve drinks."

Stephanie sighed and showed him her warrant card.

"Now, did you know Michelle?" she said again.

The barman, clearly not intimidated smiled sarcastically. "I'm new here. If you don't want a drink, you'd better see the Manager. His office is over there," he said pointing to a door.

Stephanie deposited her warrant card in the pocket of her jacket, walked across the varnished wooden floor, knocked on the door and went in without waiting for an answer.

The Manager finally finished the conversation he was having, hung up the phone and pointed to a chair.

He looked Stephanie up and down, lingering on her 34C breasts, smiling his approval. "What can I do for you?" he asked, confident in his good looks and accustomed to the attentions of the many women that ventured through his establishment. He ran a hand across his neatly trimmed goatee beard.

"Michelle Warner?"

"And you would be?" the Manager asked.

For the third time in a few minutes, Stephanie showed her warrant card. The Manager took a cursory look. "Thought you had come for a job," he smiled again, which was met by a frosty stare from the policewoman.

"Tell me about her," Stephanie asked, hopeful that she had misread his suggestive look.

He reached into his top drawer, removed a packet of cigarettes and proceeded to light one with an elegant gold lighter. "Poor girl. Sad what happened to her."

Stephanie took in the smoke and instinctively touched the nicotine patch on her arm. She had only given up the habit two weeks ago and was still fighting the temptation to restart.

"Nothing much to tell you. Michelle had been working here for three months. She was no problem, always did her shifts. In short, Michelle was a reliable girl who would always phone to say if she couldn't come in."

"Was she supposed to work over the weekend?"

"No."

"When did she last work?"

"Friday afternoon."

"The Friday she got killed?"

Stephanie could have killed him when he crushed the stub into the ashtray after only four drags.

"I presume so. Look, I told your lot all this over the phone."

Stephanie smiled sweetly, sardonically. "I know, bear with me. How much was she paid?"

"It depends."

"What do you mean?"

"I thought you knew how we operate." He paused then recited. "Okay here's how it works. The girls pay us a fee for each shift they work, they charge twenty pounds for a private dance and anything they make is theirs."

"So how much did she make a night?"

The Manager lifted his feet onto the desk, and began playing with the huge gold ring on the middle finger of his right hand. "It depends. A few hundred on a good night."

"What was her average?"

The Manager got up, went to the drinks cabinet behind him, and took out a bottle of Courvoisier and two glasses. He turned to

Stephanie "Care for a drink?" he asked, his tongue licking his lips in a deliberately flirtatious gesture.

"I think you know the answer," she replied, again ignoring the blatant come on.

He poured himself a generous glassful and took a swallow. "Hard to say; I reckon between two hundred and two fifty pounds a shift."

"How many shifts would she do in a week?"

"I'd say between six and eight."

Stephanie quickly did the calculations in her head. "So she was earning around fifteen hundred pounds a week?" Christ that's almost seventy grand a year she thought.

The Manager shrugged, "if you say so."

Stephanie looked straight into his eyes. "Do the girls offer *'personal services'* to top up their wages?" (Not that they needed topping up she thought - they were earning over twice her salary for probably half the hours and stress.)

The Manager smirked. "Officer this is a respectable club. I have a licence to protect. We operate a three-foot no touching rule," he said.

"What about outside the club?"

"Nothing like that is tolerated on our premises." He shrugged his shoulders and leant forward, "Of course should a girl make private arrangements with a customer, I wouldn't know would I?" he said in one final attempt to attract her interest.

"Did Michelle?" Stephanie pushed.

"Not to my knowledge. I've got thirty girls on the books. I don't have time to get involved with their personal lives." He took another swig of the brandy. "All I want are girls that come in when they're supposed to and stick to our rules."

"Did she have a boyfriend?"

"I don't know. I never met him if she did."

"Was she close to any of the other girls?"

"She often worked the same shifts as Lydia."

"When is Lydia next working?"

"Actually she's out there now. I'll point her out to you," he said, pleased to get rid of her now that it was obvious his advances were in vain.

They both got up and headed for the door. He had opened it and was about to follow her to the bar when the phone rang.

"Sorry I'll have to get that. She's over there by the bar," he said, pointing out the blue bikini clad Lydia before returning to his office.

Stephanie walked towards the woman who nervously lit a cigarette. "Hello Lydia. I gather you knew Michelle?" she smiled, hoping to get her to open up.

"Yes I knew her," she answered brusquely.

"What can you tell me about her?"

Lydia shrugged her shoulders and let out the smoke. "We worked together sometimes."

Once again, Stephanie touched her patch. Bloody smokers she thought to herself.

"What did you talk about?"

"This and that," she said reluctant to help.

"Can you be a little more specific?"

Lydia blew out another cloud of smoke. "Girlie things. How we hated having to do this. You know."

"Do you mind not blowing smoke in my direction Lydia?" Stephanie asked before resuming her questioning. "So why do you?"

"What do you think?" Lydia scowled.

"How long have you worked here?"

"About eight months."

"So you were here when Michelle started."

Lydia sighed, "Yes."

"Ok, so why was *she* working here?"

Lydia turned her head away from the detective, blew out another column of smoke before turning back, "same as the rest of us; she needed the money."

"She was a dancer wasn't she?"

"And?"

"So how did she end up working here?"

"Look around you. Most of us are dancers. Too many dancers, not enough shows. You spend more time auditioning than working. The bills start to pile up, you end up in a place like this."

"That's what happened to Michelle?"

"I suppose so."

"Do you know what she was doing before she started here?"

"In between jobs."

"Did she use drugs? Did she have a habit?" Stephanie asked.

"She was clean. She might smoke a spliff, but that's it."

"Was she on the game?"

"Course she wasn't."

"Did she have a boyfriend?"

"No," Lydia answered.

"What about previous boyfriends? Any of them that would have wanted her harmed?"

"She never spoke to me about any ex-boyfriends."

"Was she in any kind of trouble?"

"Not to my knowledge."

"Do you have *any* idea who could have done this?"

"No."

Stephanie decided to give up on Michelle. "Did you know Andrea Bailey?"

"Yes," Lydia replied smoothly.

"How did she meet Michelle?"

"At a bar."

"How long had they known each other?"

"About three months."

"Do you know the name of the bar where they met?"

Lydia was visibly getting agitated. "I can't remember."

"You're lying Lydia," Stephanie accused.

Lydia crossed her arms defensively which unintentionally served to push up her heaving breasts. "Am I?"

Stephanie decided to get pushy now that she realised that Lydia was getting rattled. "You'd better tell me. I'm going to find out, believe me. This is a murder case Lydia," she threatened.

Lydia bit her lip and thought for a moment before answering. "Okay. Look Michelle was gay."

The penny dropped. "Was Andrea her lover?" Stephanie asked.

Lydia smiled and clapped sarcastically, which only served to piss Stephanie off further.

"Where were you last weekend Lydia?"

Lydia realised what the policewoman was hinting at. "I didn't kill them."

"Where were you?" Stephanie repeated.

"At my parents."

Stephanie gave her a menacing glare. "You know I'm going to check."

"Whatever, I didn't do it! I've got to go now," she said and stormed off, her bum moving angrily in the tight bikini bottoms.

Marcus took a deep breath then knocked on the door. He heard footsteps followed by the sound of a chain being attached before a plump woman of around fifty opened the door just enough to allow him a sight down the hall. She looked him up and down; giving him a look Marcus had seen many times before when someone stepped in something foul.

"Is Natasha in?" he asked uneasily.

The woman ran her fingers through her damp unbrushed hair, took a last scornful look of loathing, then turned round and shouted to Natasha who appeared a few minutes later to let the chain off the hook dressed in scruffy jeans, baggy sweatshirt and socks.

She noted his stare. "I've just been studying."

"Are you busy?"

"Give me a minute to put some shoes on and I'll be over," Natasha said and scurried off back to her room.

Taff Morgan hit the buzzer and allowed the two overall clad painters inside the station.

"Thanks for coming. This shouldn't take long. We just need a written statement from both of you," he said, leading them into the interior of the station to the interview rooms. "If you'll take a seat I'll get my colleague and we can start."

Thirty minutes later Taff and Stephanie emerged from the interview rooms and headed back to their office with statements verifying that both men had left Napier Court at around 7.00 p.m. on the night Andrea Bailey was murdered. Peter Haig had dropped off his nephew Darren Turner as usual, and then proceeded home, where he spent a night in with his wife and family who could all corroborate his whereabouts. Darren had spent the night with friends in various pubs in Blackheath, getting home around midnight after seeing a girl home.

"I hope you didn't mind me knocking," Marcus said.

"If you think swotting up on molecular structure, chemical equilibria and kinetics is fun, then you are seriously wrong," said Natasha, who had changed into smarter jeans and a loose top.

"Ok. I just needed to talk to you."

Marcus turned the corkscrew, popped the cork and poured two glasses of the Australian wine he had purchased earlier in the afternoon at the local off licence. He handed Natasha one of the glasses.

The assistant from Melbourne had influenced Marcus' choice, insisting that the bottle he now placed in the fridge was an excellent wine. He hoped Natasha would appreciate his gesture.

Marcus took a sip of the wine, which was as promised seriously good. He took a deep breath, "have a seat Natasha, I want you to know about Maxine."

"You don't have to explain anything."

"Please listen," he implored, taking another slug of the wine before resuming.

"My parents are very religious. They belong to a small church – The Church of The Final Coming – that does not believe in celebrating birthdays, drinking alcohol and definitely no sex before marriage. Their whole lives belong to the Church. I mean *everything* they do is controlled by the church. TV is frowned upon because it might give conflicting views to those of the church. Contact with 'non-believers' is restricted to a minimum, so I had no friends outside of the Church."

"When my parents went back to Antigua – to prepare for His return," Marcus said dryly, "they left me with what they thought was enough money to rent a flat and look after myself for a year. After that, I was on my own. It was so strange. For all my life I had been used to looking after my parents, doing whatever they said, now all of a sudden I had to learn to live alone and find out what I wanted to do."

"Simple things such as shopping became a nightmare. I mean before it was just a case of taking the list and the money to the shops and following instructions. I never had to worry about budgeting or considering how to pay for things. Pretty soon I realised my money wouldn't last very long, so I gave up college and looked for work."

"I got a job with an insurance company. That's where I first met Maxine, she worked in the same office. We found out that her brother and I went to the same school, that's how we got talking."

"Anyway, after a while we got together. I knew nothing about women. Maxine was my first and only girlfriend. She is a 'doer'; she's three years older than I am. I think she got off on being the boss. It was Maxine that suggested we went out, decided where we went, when we should move in together and when we got a mortgage. For the first time in my life, someone else was looking after me. She quickly managed to spend the money my parents left me," Marcus said with remorse.

"I don't know why I'm telling you all this, but I feel after....well you know what happened, I think you deserve an explanation."

Natasha smiled and drank some more of the wine.

"You know what the worst thing was? It wasn't that she was unfaithful, I mean fucking someone else. I think I could have accepted, maybe even forgiven her for that. It was the fact that she couldn't tell me that she no longer loved me or cared enough for me to be honest. I meant nothing to her. "

Marcus fought back the tears. "I really like you Natasha; I want you to know that. Just give me a bit more time."

Stephanie tossed her bag onto the sofa and kicked off her shoes. The blinking light coming from the answering machine indicated she had a message. She pushed the button and listened to Tim's voice as he explained that things in the studio were hectic and he would be getting home much later than usual.

Stephanie clicked off the machine and went to the freezer. She rummaged through the various packets before finally deciding on an M & S low calorie lasagne for one.

As she popped the ready meal into the microwave, a thought came into her head.

Stephanie poured a glass of red wine and sat at the table.

A woman had made the call, how did the caller get inside the flat? Could that woman have been Lydia? She knew both of the victims. Had she been there on that night?

Taff Morgan sat between his two daughters in the busy restaurant enjoying their meal. He watched as his eldest girl raised a slice of the steak up to her mouth, the shiny gloss emphasizing her full lips.

Serena enjoyed her food and was often voicing her hatred of non-sensical diets. It showed in her figure, not that she was overweight, she was proud of her womanly curves (her own words). She chewed heartily on the meat - cooked rare - savouring the taste of blood, juices and spices.

He took a sip from his wineglass and smiled. "I'm really glad we did this."

"Me too," Serena agreed.

"I'm sorry I haven't been there for you."

Serena took her father's hand, "You don't have to apologise dad," she consoled.

"I want to. I realise I've been selfish. Whatever happened between your mother and me, I shouldn't have let it affect us."

Serena flicked her long, bright red hair from her eyes. "Are you seeing anybody?" she asked.

"Who'd have him?" Laura butted in cheekily. Whereas her sister was an avid opponent of the aesthetic, image was all-important to Laura. Her natural red hair was dyed a combination of jet-black and magenta. Like her sister, she wore shiny lip-gloss on her pale freckled face. Days at the gym, swimming, netball and dance kept the curves that her sister was so proud of at bay. Though not model-slim, Laura possessed a strong, toned, athletic body reminiscent of those triathletes she was tinkering on becoming.

"No. I'm not," said Taff.

"I think you should. You deserve to be happy."

"I am, honestly. I just want us to be close again."

Laura leaned across and kissed her father. "There's hope for you yet dad," wondering if she could persuade him to buy her a mountain bike.

Chapter 10

Marcus lay propped in bed watching a home video of a young black boy of about six playing football. The boy kicked the ball and the back of a man appeared and kicked the ball back. The man turned around and smiled joyfully as he waved to the camera.

Marcus remembered the day as if it were yesterday. He switched off the video. He had made his mind up; there was no way he was going to turn himself in. His son deserved a father.

He hadn't meant to kill her. Anyway, she couldn't have been up to any good. How did she get all that money? Moreover, why hadn't she put it in a bank? Why should he give up his life for an accident? She couldn't be brought back. What was the point in wasting so many lives – his son's, Natasha's and his own for something that could not be changed?

Natasha. How strange. Since he had allowed Natasha to get close, things were starting to feel better. It was so ironic; she epitomised the dichotomy of desire that was haunting him. He had not wanted to trust another woman after what had happened with Maxine, yet here he was, having feelings.

The truth was deep down Marcus knew he needed a woman. Brainwashed by his parents and The Church, he had genuinely believed that fornication (as his mother always referred to the act) was a sin. He had lived for eighteen years without sex – until he met Maxine. She had taught him the joys of the flesh; and she had been an excellent teacher. Since the break-up and his 'illness', he had not had a single encounter.

Now, for the first time in years, he felt human again. He deserved to be happy. If only *she* - the media had revealed her name was Andrea Bailey - hadn't come back early then she would still be alive. It was her fault.

He took stock. There was nothing to connect them. He had not been seen entering or leaving the building. He was sure he had not left any fingerprints or DNA for the forensics team to find. He had no previous, so even if they did find a print they wouldn't find it on their records. He hadn't spent any of the money or made any deposits into his bank account. How would they catch him if they had no reason to suspect him? Already the coverage on the news had scaled down, the last item on the case had only been a small piece hidden in the local rag. This was London; there was always another murder ready to grab the headlines. All he had to do was to stay calm.

Marcus rose, took a shower and washed away the last vestiges of guilt.

Claudia walked into the station, put her bags down in her office and walked along the corridor to the canteen to get a cup of coffee. On the way back she was joined by Taff and Stephanie.

"We've got some good news guv," Stephanie beamed.

"Let's have it then."

"Andrea's father. He's phoned in."

"Great!"

"Apparently he's been on holiday in Jamaica with his family for the last five weeks." Taff said. "He only learnt about the murder when he saw it in an old newspaper at work."

Claudia winced, "Nice way to find out. When's he coming in?"

"I've arranged for us to go over and see him. He's a social worker, lives in Hackney."

"Okay."

"I went to the club where Michelle worked. She was gay. I spoke to Lydia, her ex-girlfriend. I mean *friend* not lover," said Stephanie.

"Yes. Makes sense now you think about it. Neither of the girls had boyfriends. Medical reports showed signs of recent sexual activity but no semen," said Taff.

"At last we're starting to get somewhere. I thought that we might have got some information after the TV slot, but nothing of real value. It's as if Andrea hardly existed," said Claudia.

"How did Michelle meet Andrea?" Taff asked as he put his feet up on his desk.

"At some bar, Lydia's not sure where though," Stephanie replied.

"This other woman, Lydia, did she know Andrea too?" Claudia asked.

Stephanie nodded, "Yes, but she says she doesn't know who would want to kill them. She couldn't have done it; she was at her parents' over the weekend. I've checked it out."

Claudia leant back in her chair, "So what's the motive?"

"I think we can rule out a burglar, there were no signs of a forced entry. They didn't take the credit cards and as we know, Andrea had a total of over £100,000 in her bank accounts. The keys to her BMW weren't taken. Even if you assume that the person wasn't savvy enough to do something with all that, between them the two victims had over three hundred pounds in their handbags. Some piss poor burglar if he left that behind," said Taff.

"He could have got the shits and panicked," Stephanie offered.

Taff raised his eyebrows dubiously.

"Do you think it was sex? Some kind of lesbian revenge thing? Could another girl have been there?" Claudia asked Stephanie.

"I suppose it's possible."

"We'd better get in touch with the gay community, if you get my drift," said Taff.

Stephanie took a deep breath. "Guv I was thinking about the call. If it was made by a woman....."

Taff steered the unmarked car through the crowded streets of Islington, past ordinary looking yet exorbitantly priced properties that commanded prices only affordable if you were of serious standing. The pair remained silent as they drove through Upper Street, down Essex Road into Balls Pond Road and the more achievable housing to those who were prepared to accept Dalston/Kingsland as part of their home address.

Five minutes later, Claudia and Stephanie walked up the path of a well-tended garden to the door of a semi on a council estate off Mare Street in Hackney, conscious that the several owners of Staffordshire terriers that seemed to be on each corner had noted their arrival.

Taff rang the bell and the pair waited until a tall dreadlocked black man opened the door. Taff guessed him to be in his early forties despite the greying beard, though he was never sure with black people who invariably seemed to age well. Taff wondered if the PC brigade would disapprove of his stereotyping. The man who greeted the pair was wearing jeans, a red, gold and green t-shirt with a cannabis leaf motif, his toes protruding through brown leather sandals.

"Mr Clifford Williams?"

"Yes," the man nodded.

"I'm DS Morgan; this is my colleague DI St Clair."

"Hello come on in," the black man said in a faint Jamaican accent opening the door wider to allow them through.

He led them into the living room. Large framed pictures of Haile Selassie, Bob Marley and a man Taff did not recognise but Claudia knew was Marcus Garvey adorned three walls. A full size Jamaican flag of green, yellow and black covered the other wall. Pictures of Clifford Williams and his family at varying stages of their lives were proudly on view above the pine bookcase, on shelves and in the walnut display cabinet. Taff thought that this well maintained room and house did not belong on such a rough estate.

"Would you like a cup of tea or coffee?"

"If it's no trouble I'll have a coffee," Claudia smiled.

"No problem, the kettle's just boiled." He turned to Taff. "How about you Sergeant?"

"Coffee's fine thanks."

Williams nodded, left for the kitchen and returned a few minutes later with three cups on a tray. He took a seat in the armchair opposite the Welshman, the trauma of the last few days etched in his face.

"Help yourself to milk and sugar," he said wearily.

"Thank you."

The two officers added milk and sugar to their drinks.

Claudia took a sip of her coffee, "You know we are here to talk about Andrea."

"Yes. What do you want to know?"

"Mr Williams, we know that she came here to find you; how long did you know her?"

"About a year."

"How did she find you?"

"I don't know." He sipped his drink slowly. "Andrea turned up at my house one day; she asked me if I knew Thérèse Bailey. I told her I don't think so. She asked me if I'm sure. I asked her who this Thérèse Bailey was and why I should know her? She tells me that the woman was her mother and that I am her father."

"You could have knocked me over from the shock. I couldn't believe what I was hearing. I looked at her hard and realised that she wasn't some mad woman; she really meant it. I made her come inside and asked her to tell me about her mother. When she told me some more and then showed me her birth certificate, I realised who she was talking about.

He took another sip of his drink before continuing.

"She used to call herself Terri; that's why it never clicked at first. It must have been over twenty-five years ago. I met her at a jazz club, we saw each other for a few months, but it was nothing serious."

He sipped his drink again.

"I remember she came from a rich family who didn't like black people. She used to say she wished her father knew that she was sleeping with a black man."

"What happened? Why did you split up?" Claudia asked.

Williams shrugged his shoulders, "I don't know. I think we had some words; I still can't remember over what. Anyway, we both knew it wasn't a serious thing. She moved and I never saw her again."

He let out a deep breath. "When Andrea showed up, it was such a shock. I needed time to take it all in. I told her I hadn't known her mother was pregnant."

"Did Andrea believe you?"

"I don't think she did at first. She said she had to go, but asked if she could see me again. I told her yes, but not here. I have a wife and kids you see."

"So what happened when you saw her the next time?"

Williams finished his drink and placed the empty cup on the tray.

"We met at a Macdonald's," he smiled at the memory. "She liked burgers; she must have eaten about four of them. She wanted to know about me and her mother, so I told her what happened."

"How did she react?" asked Claudia.

"She was fine. She asked me about myself, what I did, what I was like when I was younger? I told her. She asked about my family," he pointed to one of the family pictures, "I've got three kids by my wife; two girls and a boy. She wanted to know how long I've been married and looked happy when I told her twenty-three years."

He paused. "Would you like another cup of coffee?"

"Thank you."

"Yes please."

Williams went to the kitchen and came back with fresh cups and an assortment of biscuits. He settled back down in his chair.

Claudia bit on a chocolate biscuit and washed it down with some of the coffee before asking, "You were saying Mr Williams?"

"Right. We saw each other again. She asked more about the kids; wanted to know all about them. She was really pleased, said it was strange to know that she had a little brother and sisters; how she'd always wanted a brother."

He reached across to the plate and picked up a ginger nut biscuit, took a bite and a gulp of his coffee before continuing.

"Then she asks if she can meet them. I told her that I'd have to talk to everybody. She said she really wanted to meet them; after all, they were her family. She begged me to arrange it."

He took another drink from his cup.

"I had to tell my wife. That was hard. To tell her I had another child – and from a white girl! She went crazy. At first, she said no, but I eventually managed to talk her round. I told her we *had* to tell the kids, that they had a right to know. So we talked to them and they agreed they wanted to see her. So my wife cooked a special dinner and I brought Andrea round." He smiled.

"What's so funny?" Taff asked.

"No I was just remembering that dinner. You see, Andrea didn't know anything about West Indian food. She kept asking what everything was."

He looked across to Claudia who nodded her understanding.

"Poor girl didn't know what she was eating, but she still ate it. Everything went well. My wife and the kids liked her. The wife felt sorry for her and told her she must come round again."

"And did she?"

"Yes about three more times."

"When did you last see her?" Taff asked.

"About three months ago."

"Why did she stop coming round?" Claudia asked.

Williams took a deep breath and shook his head.

"One day she phoned and said she wanted to see me. I told her to come round, but she said she couldn't and tells me to meet her at a bar in Richmond. I did. She turned up in a flash BMW and drove me to her flat in Chiswick."

"Chiswick you said?" asked Taff.

"Yes that's right."

"Do you know the address?"

"No. All I know was that it was really nice, classy."

"Do you know when she moved?"

Williams shook his head. "I didn't even know she had until I read that paper."

"Why did she leave without telling you?"

Williams closed his eyes as he spoke, I'll explain.

Andrea turned the key in the lock, pushed open the door and ushered Williams inside the spacious expensive flat. Williams' eyes opened in awe at the impressive sight that greeted him. Andrea smiled sweetly.

"Let me take your coat dad."

She took Williams' coat and moved into the hallway. Williams was still taking it all in when Andrea returned. She was wearing a short black Dolce & Gabbana dress that showed off all the curves of her body and left little to the imagination. Some clearly expensive jewellery completed the outfit.

She held up a large bottle of brandy and a Magnum of champagne.

"Get comfortable dad," she smiled.

She worked the cork from the champagne bottle expertly, poured out two drinks, walked over and handed one to Williams, who had taken a seat in a soft leather settee. Andrea sat beside him.

"Only the best for you dad."

She clinked glasses and smiled at Williams. "Do you know it's funny, I'm twenty-five years old and only just learning to say 'dad'."

Williams placed his arms around his daughter, "Don't worry, we can make up for lost time."

The smile dropped from Andrea's face as she recoiled from his touch. "Aren't you curious about how I can afford to live like this dad?" Only 'dad' is now starting to sound like a pretty menacing word.

"It's none of my business."

"Guess dad," she implored.

"I don't know. Money from your mother's family I suppose?"

Andrea stood up, fixing Williams with a stare that he cannot escape from, not the look that a daughter should be giving her father. She slowly pulled up the short dress to reveal that she was naked underneath.

"Fucking men!" Andrea spat, full of spite. "That's what pays for it all."

97

She pulled the dress down and when he looked at her, Williams saw the extent of her animosity in her eyes.

"That's exactly what she said – "Fucking men," Williams said as the tears trickled down his creased black face. He continued to describe events of that night through tears.

"I'm good you know. That's what they all tell me." Andrea said looking at Williams with disgust. "Oh you're so fucking good," she mimicked a man's voice. She stopped, the edge returning in her voice. "But I should be shouldn't I; I've had enough practice. I've been fucking men since I was ten," she shouted now clearly out of control. "Yes ten dad," *she spat, making the word sound like an insult, "that's how old I was when my uncle started abusing me!"*

Williams, at a loss at what to do or how to react; witnessed the whole episode in silent horror.

"Where were you then dad? *How come you were there for your black kids? Wasn't I black enough for you? Is that what was wrong with me?"*

"I didn't know Andrea, on my children's lives," Williams pleaded, without realising what an inappropriate choice of phrase he had just made. Andrea leapt to her feet and began punching and lashing out wildly, then grabbing his arms and dragging Williams to his feet.

"Get out of my flat and get the fuck out of my life! I don't need you. You're like all the rest of them. Fucking men! Go on get out!!" Andrea screamed hysterically

"Jesus!" was all that Taff could muster.

Williams shook his head, trying to keep in control, but failing as he sobbed. "I didn't know, I really didn't."

Chapter 11

Marcus and Natasha sat together on the sofa. Cans of beer rested at their feet as the Rare Groove tape played LaToya Jackson's *Kamp Kuchi Kaia.*

Natasha took a drag from the spliff. She turned to Marcus, "Don't you miss your son?"

"Of course I do." God how did she know that had been on his mind recently?

"When did you last see him?"

Marcus swallowed the beer, "Over a year now."

"I think you should get in touch with him. It's not his fault."

She passed him the spliff.

"I tried. It's just not fair on him, putting him through the grief. You don't understand."

Natasha was hurt. "Don't keep saying that. Okay I haven't got a kid, but I know what it's like to miss a parent. I had to watch my mother get more and more depressed."

She cracked open a can of beer, took a swig then continued. "It got so bad that sometimes I didn't dare go out and leave her alone. Then she killed herself; after everything I had done. I used to wonder what I'd done to make her stop loving me; thinking why wasn't I enough for her? It should have been dad she hated; *he* had the affair."

"I'm sorry I never thought."

She took his hand. "Don't feel sorry. I don't anymore. I have to live with what has happened and so do you. Do something about it."

"His mother won't allow it."

"Well at least try. Fight for him; don't just give up."

"What's it to you?"

"For Christ's sakes Marcus, I care about you. You know that."

Marcus shook his head. "Why?"

"Because you're a decent caring person."

"You don't know anything about me."

"What I know I like. When you're ready to tell me more you will. I can wait," Natasha said gently.

Marcus looked into her eyes, "I wish I could have met you when I was a human being."

Natasha whacked him. "Stop saying that."

She accepted the spliff as the music changed and Teddy Prendergrass' *Close the door* began playing.

"Sorry," Marcus said apologetically.

"Stop it," she ordered.

She turned to him and kissed him. Marcus returned her kiss and felt her arms wrapping round his body. His fingers ran through her hair as he took in her scent. Natasha placed his hands on her breasts, urging him to caress them. Marcus closed his eyes; it felt so good. His breathing became heavier as Natasha placed her tongue inside his mouth and started to stroke the outline of his cock.

Natasha stood up slowly, taking him by his hand and leading him to the bed. She pushed him gently onto the bed and started to undress; watching his reaction as she discarded every item of clothing until she stood naked in front of him.

Despite his state of arousal, Marcus noted she had not a tattoo in sight. He groaned as she knelt down and started unbuttoning his shirt, tenderly kissing his chest as she loosened each button. She unzipped his jeans, tugged them from his body, tossed them to the floor and joined him on the bed.

Claudia St Clair and her husband were getting ready for bed. Ken walked through to the en-suite bathroom and started brushing his teeth. Claudia tied the sash of the silk kimono as she sat on the chair in front of the dresser mirror removing her make up.

"Have they told you anything more?" Ken called from the bathroom.

"No."

"When do you think we'll find out?"

"When a post comes up."

"It's bloody ridiculous. How are we supposed to make plans?"

"We've been through this before Ken."

"Yes I know, and it never ceases to amaze me how unprofessional the police are."

He walked back into the bedroom and got into bed. "What's going to happen if you're posted out of London?"

"I don't know. Why what do you think? We've managed up till now."

"That was different Claudia. I can't relocate this time."

"Can't or won't?"

Ken fluffed his pillow and tried to find a comfortable position. "Okay, both. You know how important it is for me to be in London with what's happening in the company."

She finished and joined him in bed. "So I'm supposed to sacrifice my career?"

"Would it be such a bad thing?"

"I can't believe you said that."

Ken rested on one elbow and looked at his wife. "Why? Don't say I'm being selfish."

"My job is just as important as yours Ken. Okay so you make lots of money and keep people in jobs, I'll not deny you that. Do you know that today I met a man whose daughter has been murdered? How do you think that felt Ken? I have to catch that murderer."

"All very noble Claudia, but when does it stop? What about us? Is everybody else more important than we are? **We** agreed we wanted a family. You can't keep putting it off every time there's a murder or you get promoted."

"Let's see where I get posted," Claudia ended, turning away from her husband.

Natasha was asleep in Marcus' bed, her arm draped around his shoulder, when his writhing and tossing about woke her. She shook him awake.

"What's the matter?" Natasha asked, the concern visible in her face.

"Sorry. It was just a bad dream."

What about?

"It's nothing," he said, wiping the sweat from his forehead.

"Tell me. Was it about her?"

"No. It was just a bad dream."

Natasha brought her hand to his face. "What happened between you and her?"

Now awake, Marcus raised himself up in the bed. "What's to tell? We got married and had a child. She fucked around, divorced me, took me for everything and won't let me see my son."

Natasha reached up and kissed him. Little soft kisses, "you poor thing," she consoled.

"Yes, well that was when I was a human being."

Natasha punched his shoulder. "Don't say that. Don't let her win," she implored.

"It's so hard. I lost everything. Not just possessions; I mean my pride, respect and self-confidence. She stripped me of it all. I used to ask myself what *I* had done wrong. Then you find you're questioning everything you do and believing that you **did** do something wrong, before you know it you don't trust yourself or anybody else. All I ever wanted was someone that would be honest, someone I could trust."

Natasha stroked his chest affectionately.

"You asked me before why I moved to Blackheath remember?"

Natasha nodded.

"After she kicked me out, I lost it. I had nowhere to go. At first, I stayed with the few friends I had until I could see that I was overstaying my welcome. When people ask you to stay as long as it takes, they don't mean it literally."

"I didn't know what to do, where to turn for help. I slept in my car until the money ran out and I had to sell it. Then I walked the streets for weeks until an Outreach Worker who had seen me about and was worried about me approached me. Anyway, to cut a long story short, I was diagnosed as having a breakdown."

"In the end, they referred me to a hospital and kept me in for twelve weeks. That was icing on the cake for Maxine. It provided the evidence that she took to the courts to show that I couldn't cope and was not the type of person to be trusted looking after our; rather *her* son. She was right. If I had been stronger then I would not have crumbled."

"Marcus, stop it. Before I met you, my life was shit. I didn't have a life! Look at me; I'm twenty-three and still living at 'home' with my dad who I don't get on with anymore, and a bitch that I hate."

"I was wondering about that. Why don't you move out?" Marcus said, forgetting about himself for a moment.

"And go where? I have to work like a slave just to get through Uni. I can't afford to rent a flat in London that's going to be empty half the year on my own."

"You must have friends?"

"Have I? No one I can talk to. Why do you think I knocked on your door? We'd only said hello a few times before."

"Why me?" Marcus asked.

"I don't know," she traced a finger over Marcus' face. "You lived next door I suppose, plus you looked like you would listen."

Natasha sat up in the bed, her breasts jiggling as she leant over to retrieve the spliff from the ashtray.

"Do you know what my surname is?"

Marcus shook his head.

She lit the spliff, took a drag, "Buck, Natasha B-U-C-K. You can imagine the stick I got at school. I soon learned that staying in the background and not drawing attention to myself often saved me from being picked on. I guess I recognised something in you. That you would understand what it felt like."

She cuddled close to him. "Whatever it was, I'm glad I did. We've got each other now."

Taff cradled the phone between his neck and shoulder as he reached for his mug of coffee. After a couple of rings, a young teenage girl answered.

"Hi Bella speaking, can I help you?"

"Hello Bella, this is Sergeant Morgan, how's your brother and his arm?"

"Oh he's fine. Loving the attention he's getting of course. Men, they are soooo weak."

Taff coughed. "Is your mother there please?"

"I'll just get her."

Taff heard the footsteps fade away, followed a short while later by the sound of a more mature female voice. "Hello Sergeant, what can I do for you?"

"Sorry to disturb you Mrs Wilkes, but something's been troubling me. I had a feeling there was something you weren't telling us when we met."

"As I said, it was just rumours. You know what people in small places are like."

This was too fluffy for Taff, who cleared his throat as a preparation for getting some hard facts out of all this. She'd wound him up with her hints. He wanted it straight.

"Was it something to do with the Bailey family? "he asked.

"Oh God!" said Sally, "this isn't London. Round here, word gets around and rumours spread. I can't be the one to tell you!"

"You've got to Mrs Wilkes, you may be able to help us find Andrea's killer" said Taff.

"Google it up," Sally said after a long moment's consideration.

"Pardon?"

"Google up the name Piers Bailey and Exeter Weekly Chronicle on the computer. After that, I'm sorry but I don't want to get involved; I mean that in the nicest possible way," she added; ending the conversation.

Five minutes later Taff came back from the toilet, made sure his flies were correctly buttoned, and then reached out to pick up the ringing phone.

"I've just been on the phone to my husband, he says it's pathetic to drop hints and withhold the kind of information I know you were hoping to get OK? By the way, he's the Vicar here. He was a teacher when we married. He was always too sensitive to deal with the raging hormones of teenagers and they knew it too. Anyway deep down he knew that this is what he wanted; so here I am the vicar's wife."

"We bought this place when it was badly run down, worked very hard getting it right and we didn't want to move into the vicarage in the town. That was my fault. I wouldn't go. The children loathed the place, it's horrible, you could never get it warm and it's got rats. Anyway he thinks I should tell you everything we know, 'leave out the rumours – just the facts and let you put two and two together' he said."

Taff waited patiently for her to get to the point.

"Piers Bailey is –was – Andrea's uncle. To his credit, he was always there for his sister and her child. He was the chief link between them and the rest of the family. At the time, Thérèse lived in a small cottage her mother had inherited that her father let out as a holiday place. It didn't do very well, because we aren't right on the sea here, so old man Bailey wasn't doing himself down much, letting Andrea have it. God! I bet he even got paid through Housing Ben...," she stopped herself.

"Got the picture," Taff nodded solemnly as he doodled a set of random lines on his blotter, "in any case that would be a matter of record."

"Quite. Well, Piers worked a lot from home; he was an IT consultant. He also gave piano lessons, mostly to local kids; led music projects in Summer Play schemes and that kind of stuff. The thing is, he was sent to prison two years ago for downloading child porn on the internet and two charges of … child molestation," Sally blushed.

Taff sat up in his chair.

Sally continued, "He was part of a ring that had strong links with Cardiff and Bristol. There were also others in various parts of the country as I recall. The police had been investigating for years, but they said Piers had been very clever. He pleaded guilty in the end though. Two other men got longer sentences, but they weren't tried together so there wasn't much about them in the local papers."

She added, "The offences had begun five years earlier; the victims were two girls aged thirteen and ten."

Taff pulled open the bottom drawer of his desk and found the bottle of Glenfiddich. He tossed the dregs of his coffee into the bin, poured out a large shot and downed it in one. Jesus why did he have to be the one to tell Claudia this?

Marcus took one final look at the list he had compiled to make sure he had not forgotten anything. It read, baby oil, baby lotion, after-shave, cocoa butter, Vaseline, cotton buds and deodorant, items that Maxine would always keep a plentiful stock of in the bathroom cupboard. He glanced out of the window, decided it was warm enough to go without a jacket, left the newly cleaned bed-sit and made his way out of Lambton House.

Remembering the promise he had made to himself, he kept his head up as he walked. He took a sharp intake of breath as an old lady walking her two small dogs approached. "Good morning," he said nervously.

She looked at him and smiled without a hint of fear or unease. "Good morning to you too. Lovely day isn't it?"

"Yes. Well have a nice time," Marcus replied.

"Thank you very much, young man," the lady said and continued on her way.

And that was it; his first conversation with a real stranger for ages. Okay, so it had only been brief, but it was a start. Marcus smiled, took a deep breath and continued walking. As he approached the entrance to the market, he witnessed a woman impatiently replace a dummy in the mouth of the young baby in the pushchair, then turn around to yank her other child angrily to her side as he fell behind her pace.

"Dante I told you not to dawdle. I've got things to do," she shouted in frustration.

Marcus stared at the young mixed-race boy, whose face perfectly demonstrated his unhappiness, and automatically thought of Monju. For a moment he contemplated approaching the young boy and comforting him; letting the young mother know how lucky she was to have him. But he quickly revised his actions when he remembered just how stubborn Monju could be when he was in 'one of those moods' and had stretched his patience to the limit. Don't be quick to judge he reminded himself as the mother struggled to fold the buggy, pick up the baby and shepherd 'Dante' onto the waiting bus.

Claudia and Stephanie sat at the bar of Tiberius Gentleman's club beside a nervous cigarette smoking Lydia.

"Lydia this is my boss DI St Clair. You haven't told us everything have you?" Stephanie said in her most assertive tone.

"I don't know what you're talking about," replied Lydia, nervously picking at her lip.

"Well let's see. How about beginning with Andrea being on the game?"

"I didn't know."

"Lydia don't lie to me again," Stephanie warned the shaken Lydia.

"Okay so I knew. I didn't want to get involved okay."

Claudia rested her hand on Lydia's shoulder. "This is a murder enquiry Lydia. You **are** involved. I suggest you tell us all you know."

"How did she operate? Did she have a pimp?" Stephanie asked.

"No. She advertised in the papers; the personal columns."

"How long had she been doing it?"

"A couple of years I think."

"Was Michelle on the game as well?" Stephanie asked

"No."

"You're not lying to me again are you Lydia?"

"No. It's the truth."

"Did you know **any** of Michelle's previous girlfriends?"

Lydia dropped the cigarette to the floor and ground it out. "She told me about a couple of girls. They lived out in the sticks. She was careful. She didn't want her family to find out she was gay."

"Was she still seeing either of them?"

"No. They happened a long time ago. Besides she didn't sleep around like that."

"What about Andrea?" asked Claudia.

"I was the only other woman Andrea had ever been with; that's how she met Michelle," Lydia finally confessed wearily.

"You used to go out with Andrea?"

Lydia broke down and started to sob. "Yes, I loved them both."

"Why didn't you tell me this before?"

"I didn't want to get involved. I didn't do it," she wept.

"Lydia, do you have any idea who could have done it?" Claudia asked consolingly.

"No. Honest I don't."

"You don't think this was some jealous lesbian thing, someone with a grudge?"

"No."

"Could it have been one of Andrea's clients?"

"She was careful. She had been badly beaten up once before and didn't take risks. She always made sure she knew who she was dealing with. She would always meet them in a public place the first time before deciding if she would take them on."

Stephanie wondered how Lydia knew so much about Andrea's business. She let it go. "Lydia, did you make the call to the police telling them about the bodies?" she asked.

Marcus opened the cupboard and took out the packet of rice, poured some into the Tupperware bowl and began washing it under the tap. Natasha walked up behind him and wrapped her arm around his waist. She took a piece of meat from the pan and popped it in her mouth. She fanned her mouth as the heat hit her tongue.

"Mmmm, this is lovely. Where did you learn to cook?"

"My mother, she made sure I was able to take over full household duties from her as soon as I reached eleven. Ironing, washing, cleaning; I did it all."

Natasha stared hard at Marcus. The change in him was incredible. She hadn't realised before, but now she could see a glow in him – not just attributable to the baby lotion and other creams he was now regularly applying. There was a new sense of purpose about him.

"Do you fancy going out tonight?" she asked suddenly.

"I don't know," Marcus said, stirring the meat with a wooden spatula.

She bit his ear. "Come on let's have some fun. We deserve it."

She opened the fridge, took out a bottle of wine, poured two glasses and handed him one.

"Thanks."

"It'll do you good to get out."

"Alright you win," Marcus said as Natasha returned to nibbling his ears.

He finished transferring the rice to a pan, placed it on the cooker then turned around and kissed her.

"Dinner will be ready in ten minutes."

"Good. Just enough time," she smiled wickedly.

"Time for what?"

Natasha put down her glass on the table and began to unzip his flies. Her eyes remained on his as she knelt to take him in her mouth.

Claudia swivelled on her chair and faced her Sergeant. "Taff?"

"We've got the statements from the decorators. One of them says he saw a black man going up the stairs on the Friday the girls were killed."

"Did he give us a description?"

"Afraid not. He only got a glimpse. Couldn't tell what he looked like, only that he was black."

"Well you'd better go through the...."

Taff held up a batch of files in anticipation of her request. "There are five I think we need to speak to."

"Okay." She turned to the policewoman. "Stephanie?"

"I thought about what you said earlier – you know, "everybody has a mobile these days", and after a stiff talk Lydia admitted taking them. Andrea advertised in contact magazines, gave her mobile number of course. Lydia ditched the SIM cards, but we managed to retrieve some numbers that had been stored in the phone. I called some of the numbers; they were not keen on talking at first. She also advertised on the internet - Lydia had her laptop too, which the techies are dealing with to see if they can access her e-mails and messages. It seems she targeted wealthy middle-aged businessmen."

Taff looked at Claudia. "That's why Ms Fawcett thought her father was white."

Stephanie looked puzzled. "What?"

"One of Andrea's neighbours saw her with a white man on a couple of occasions." Claudia explained.

Stephanie clicked. "She mistook Andrea's client for her father."

"Seems so. At first I wondered if it was her grandfather."

"Doesn't bring us any closer to finding the killer. It could have been any one of her clients. She'd been on the game for at least two years." Stephanie stated.

"Did she make any calls that night?"

"None."

"Well I suppose we're going to have to track down as many of her tricks as we can."

Claudia nodded. "Okay, Taff I want you to deal with that. Stephanie and I'll go back down to Cornwall."

Taff winced. "I don't think it would be a good idea for you to go down there boss."

"Why not? I want to hear what Bailey's got to say."

"I know, but he won't co-operate if he sees you. This man is a real chauvinist guv. He was a major in the army, a retired solicitor who established a chain of offices – he's still on the board. He likes to be in control and he won't take kindly to feeling inferior to a woman – yet alone dare I say it guv - a *black* woman."

"Well fuck him. He's going to have to learn to like it," Claudia snarled angrily.

"Why don't I go down with someone?" Stephanie suggested.

"Let her go guv. She can handle him and at least he'll talk to her." Taff sucked in a big mouthful of air, "There's something more you need to know guv," he said.

Claudia turned towards the Welshman.

"After our visit with Mr Williams, I spoke to Andrea's old teacher – a Mrs Sally Wilkes. Bailey's son is inside serving time for sex offences."

Claudia and Taff left the flat in Lambton House and looked at each other.

"I think we can rule him out," Taff said disappointedly.

"Bloody waste of time," Claudia added.

"We're not getting any closer to solving this."

"There must be something we're missing, something we just can't see."

"Yeah, who bloody well did it!" Taff answered wryly.

As they turned to walk up the next flight of stairs, Claudia stopped her Sergeant. "Taff, you're an experienced copper, how many murders have you worked on?

"Loads."

"How many unsolved?"

"A few. Five or six I should think."

"Why couldn't you solve them?"

Taff shrugged. "Usual reasons; some we knew who did it but couldn't get the evidence to prove it, others we couldn't tie it to anyone we had in the frame. Thing is guv, this looks like a one off. I don't think whoever did this has killed before and I doubt if they have form. We've nothing to cross reference this with."

"I think we're missing something."

"Taff looked at his watch. "Do you want to see this last man today? It's getting a bit late."

"What do you want to do?"

"Let's leave it till tomorrow," he said, grateful that he didn't have to walk another flight of stairs.

"Come on then."

Chapter 12

Marcus and Natasha entered the crowded nightclub to be greeted by the blaring sound system that was playing *Cosmic Lust* by Mass Production. Natasha walked to the cloakroom and handed in her coat, leaving her in a pair of black hipsters and a silver shiny crop top. She accepted her ticket, returned to the main hall where she spotted Marcus, who was waiting beside the bar.

She looked at him lovingly as she walked across to join him, noting the three black women that she saw eyeing him up. She couldn't blame them; he looked good enough to eat in a pair of dark trousers and a turquoise shirt. As he handed her a glass, she gave him a kiss to demonstrate that he was taken to the three on looking women and smiled triumphantly when he returned her kiss.

The music changed and *Living in a world of magic* by The Investigators came on. Natasha pulled Marcus to the dance floor and began dancing suggestively in front of him to the reggae tune. Halfway into the song she threw her hands over his shoulders, kissed him and ground her body into his.

Marcus and Natasha laughed merrily outside his bed-sit door. It had been a great night, the first fun night out that both had enjoyed in a long time. Marcus opened the door and the couple burst inside. Natasha reached out and kissed him lustfully.

"Can I stay over? Natasha whispered.

"Yes please," Marcus said, hungrily returning her kisses.

"I hoped you'd say that." She opened her bag, reached in and bought out a toothbrush. She tossed her bag onto the sofa, stepped out of her trousers and pulled the shiny top over her head.

"Come here!" she called wickedly.

Taff Morgan parked the unmarked police car outside Lambton House, waited for Claudia to join him before they walked the stairs and rang the bell of the bed-sit.

"Mr Carpenter?" Taff asked when Marcus opened the door.

111

"Yes."

Taff opened his wallet and showed his card. "DS Morgan. This is my colleague DI St Clair. We'd just like to ask you a few questions if you don't mind."

"Okay," Marcus said and ushered the pair inside.

"Did you know either of the murder victims?"

"No. I told the other officers I didn't."

"That's right. But you had seen them in the pub before?"

"The black one I'd seen a couple of times."

"Can you remember what you were doing that Friday?" Claudia asked.

"I was here watching TV."

"You seem pretty certain Mr Carpenter."

"I always watch TV on Friday nights."

"Were you alone?"

"Yes."

Claudia looked towards the window. "Did you look out of the window that night?" she asked.

Marcus caught her glance. "No."

"You're quite sure?"

"Yes."

Claudia stood up and walked to the window. "Do you see what I'm getting at Mr Carpenter?"

"No," Marcus lied with conviction.

"You don't?"

Taff watched on.

"No," Marcus repeated.

Claudia made a show of moving the curtains before taking a long look out of the window then said, "You get a very good view of Napier Court from here."

She locked eyes with Marcus who held her accusing stare.

"So if you were looking out of the window, you might have seen something important and not realised it," Claudia smiled.

"I'm sorry, I didn't see anything."

"How about when you closed your curtains?"

"Pardon?"

"When I close my curtains at night, I usually have a quick look around to check everything's okay," Claudia explained.

"Well I don't," Marcus said testily.

Claudia persisted. "Did you *ever* see Miss Bailey at her window?"

"No."

Claudia smiled, "Come on, not even once?"

Taff sat uncomfortably in the sofa.

Marcus fixed her an angry stare but answered calmly, "Why would I? I don't spend my time staring at others."

Claudia noted his reaction. "I'm sorry; I didn't mean to upset you. I was just thinking that perhaps you *might* have seen her with someone before. You *might* have seen her with someone who may be able to help us; someone who may have killed her; someone **you** might be able to describe to us."

"I'm sorry but I can't help you," Marcus said and exchanged another angry glance with Claudia.

She turned to Taff, who took the hint.

"Can you remember what you watched on TV that Friday Mr Carpenter?" Taff asked.

"Yes. I always watch *Adult Talk* on Fridays."

Taff nodded. "Me too. Can you remember what it was about?"

"Actually I can." Marcus said and glared at DI St Clair, "it was about men surviving in the modern world. How their roles were being lost and whether there would be a backlash."

"Thank you Mr Carpenter," said Taff looking at Claudia. "Anything else guv?"

"No. I don't think so."

Taff rose from the sofa. "Well thanks again for your help Mr Carpenter."

Claudia followed behind her colleague, just before going out of the door, she turned to Marcus. "If you should remember anything, don't hesitate to contact me."

They stared at each other again. Marcus knew that this was not an invitation but a challenge; letting him know that she didn't believe him. Marcus closed the door after her, smiled then walked to the window.

"What did you make of that?" Claudia asked Taff as they walked down the stairs.

"Not much help."

"Did you believe him?"

"About what?"

"Didn't you notice his reaction when I went to the window?"

113

Taff shook his head. "Must have missed it."

"No. His body language changed. He's not telling us something."

"Probably didn't like being accused of being a peeping Tom," Taff said, remembering vividly the first time they had clashed over the word Tom.

"That's not what I meant," Claudia said defensively.

"*I* know guv, but I don't think *he* did."

"I don't know; I've got a feeling about him."

Claudia got in the car, buckled her seatbelt and looked up to see Marcus staring down at her from his window.

Marcus watched the police car drive away. Five minutes later the bell rang and he opened the door to Natasha who was wearing a long olive green denim skirt and matching top. She gave him a kiss hello.

"Doing anything special?"

"No."

She pressed her body into his. "Good. Come on we're going into town."

"Remember *I'm* taking the lead," Stephanie instructed the male colleague that had accompanied her from London as they approached the house. She rang the bell and followed Bailey inside.

"How can I help you this time officer?" Bailey said politely addressing Stephanie's male colleague.

"Just a few more questions" Stephanie replied.

He sat in the leather armchair without offering the two detectives a seat. "Well you'd better fire away then."

No offer of drinks this time Stephanie noted. She took a seat in defiance of Bailey's conceit. "Did you know where Andrea lived in London?"

"No. I told you before that I never heard from her after she left."

"So you didn't know where she worked?"

Bailey sighed. "No."

"Or what she did for a living?"

114

"No officer. I knew neither where she lived or worked. I think we've established that now don't you?" he said pompously.

"Would it surprise you to learn that Andrea was a prostitute?"

Bailey crossed his legs, "Why was she?"

Stephanie struggled to control the animosity she felt towards the loathsome prick and continued. "Yes she was Mr Bailey."

"I'm sorry to hear that."

"How did she get on with the rest of your family?"

Bailey smoothed a crease in his trousers. "Andrea was not a sociable girl."

"Did she get on with your son?"

Bailey did not miss a beat. "I can't really say she did. Look constable, I am not going to apologise if that's what you're after. We never created the situation, but we dealt with it as we saw fit. Is that a crime?"

Stephanie noted his unease. "Did your son know where Andrea lived?"

"No."

The bastard's lying she thought. "You're certain?"

"I'm positive," Bailey answered petulantly.

Stephanie knew there was something wrong. "Does he live locally?"

"No," he snapped.

"Can you tell us where we can get hold of him?" Stephanie smiled.

"He's in prison," Bailey said, openly angry now.

"I'm sorry to hear that. What is he in prison for?"

Bailey was almost ready to blow. "I'd prefer not to discuss it thank you Constable."

"Actually it's *Detective* constable Mr Bailey" Stephanie continued, delighting in his unease. "Mr Bailey, did you know that Andrea found her father before she died? "she asked innocently.

"No I didn't."

Stephanie smiled. "Well she did. She told him all about your family; about your son."

Bailey rose to his feet unable to contain himself any longer. "If you don't mind officer I've no wish to answer any further questions without the presence of my solicitor. I think you'd better leave."

Stephanie stood up. "I think I learned what I needed to sir, thank you for your time." She held out her hand and watched his face turn red in anger.

On the way across the gravel path to the car, Stephanie's colleague turned to her and said, "Why didn't you ask him about the abuse?"

Stephanie looked in the driver's mirror and watched as Bailey angrily punched numbers into his mobile. "I didn't need to, he already knew."

Wendy sniggered merrily as she brought her wine glass to her lips. She enviously took in Natasha who was dressed in the blue Suzi Wong silk dress she had splashed out on for her second real date with Marcus. "Going out with your darkie boyfriend?"

Natasha let the slight pass without comment, happy in the knowledge that she felt gorgeous and nothing was going to dampen her mood. All her efforts were concentrated on the night ahead. Imagine; they were going to have a proper romantic date. Marcus had booked a restaurant and invited her out for a meal.

The time she had spent with Marcus recently was leading her to realize that her previous lack of confidence had blighted her love life. As a result, she had set herself up for the bad experiences. No more of that, she thought.

Claudia and Taff waited patiently as the Prison Officer selected a key from the leather pouch on her waist and finally pushed the heavy gates open. They followed silently as they were ushered into a small interview room.

"Stephanie wouldn't like this," Claudia muttered to Taff.

Taff had to agree. Stephanie had her core of steel, but he reckoned she'd have started chanting before they'd been more than five yards behind the walls.

Taff himself had never quite hardened to the prison environment. They had handed in their money, their bits and pieces (they'd let Taff keep the cigarettes which were often a vital bargaining counter with inmates of course) but it was the dreadful heavy clanging of endless gates and doors, all relocked behind them as they penetrated the depths of this gruesome old city centre prison, that made you panic.

Piers Bailey sat proudly erect in the wooden chair, his prison issue shirt and grey trousers immaculately ironed, oozing self-importance. This was no furtive little dirty-mackintosh nonce. Piers Bailey had inherited both his looks and manner from his father. Stunningly handsome, a clean-jawed, tall and authoritative man, he raised a hand to the swelling under his left eye, which was turning a nasty shade of blue. His chair was pushed back from the Formica table to give him the legroom he needed. His green eyes stared coldly at the two officers.

How arrogant was that? Like the presiding bloody officer at a court martial, Taff thought.

"You understand why we are here to speak to you?" Claudia asked.

"Actually no I don't," Bailey answered, though he might as well have said "fuck you".

"Well let me enlighten you. Your niece Andrea; when was the last time you saw her?"

"I haven't seen Andrea since her mother's funeral."

"I understand you had a special relationship with her. It seems strange you never kept in touch."

"Look, if you have anything specific to ask me then do so, otherwise I'd like to return to my cell," Bailey said without missing a beat.

Claudia told herself; "Step back, step back."

"Okay, did you know that Andrea has been murdered?"

Something stirred behind the eye that was still fully open. Then Piers made a show of studying his fingernails. "I don't read the newspapers in here."

"Didn't your father let you know?"

"I'm sure the Deputy Governor will tell you who my visitors have been, and no doubt give you details as to the contents of my mail."

"Or you could just tell us."

"Very well, no, my father did not tell me. If you persist in asking me irrelevant questions Inspector, I'm afraid I **will** end this now."

"Okay, let's talk about the offences you were convicted of."

"Do you know what a *Bat mitzvah* is Inspector?"

Claudia made a puzzled frown.

Bailey smiled. "In Judaism at a certain age a female attends a coming of age ceremony. A ceremony to signify that she is no longer a girl, but is now considered a woman."

"What the hell has that got to do...."

Bailey interrupted her and continued coolly. "The *Bat mitzvah* ceremony takes place on her *thirteenth* birthday. In certain European countries, the age of consent is fourteen Inspector. Or what about Asian arranged marriages when the bride can be even younger?"

"So why did you plead guilty?" Claudia spat, barely able to contain disgust for the man.

Bailey raised a hand and ran it through his hair. "I am here because I was advised to plead guilty for technical reasons and expediency. In law I am guilty, so I shall serve my time as I am duly obliged to do. However I have no obligation or wish to answer any further questions from you," and with that, rose from his chair.

Natasha stepped off the bus and waited for Marcus. Without asking, she slipped her hand into his and led him towards a nearby clothes shop. It was to be the first of many as the day was spent going in and out of shops, trying on clothes until Natasha finally acceded to Marcus' wish and they found a pub.

Marcus walked to the bar and waited to be served whilst Natasha took the bags and found a table. He gave the barman his order and looked around to see where Natasha was. Out the corner of his eye, he noticed the two detectives that had called at his flat seated at a table. Marcus smiled at the black woman, who returned his smile and raised her glass in recognition. Marcus paid for the drinks and joined Natasha.

Piers Bailey waited for the cell door to slam shut. He found the remote and turned on the TV in time to catch the start of his favourite Australian soap. He hopped onto his bed and smiled. The girls all looked so pure, so innocent. What did that black bitch know? Just look at those girls on the screen, their pert breasts proudly displayed in miniscule bikinis or seductive school uniforms.

He smiled. Andrea had been like that, developing early, her uniform unable to hide her ripening body. She had welcomed his affection. He more than anyone else had shown her love; theirs had been a truly special relationship. She would never have betrayed him would she? No, it was impossible. He put the thought out of his mind and concentrated on the television.

The alarm clock on the bedside table sounded. Marcus stretched out an arm and turned it off. He attempted to slip out from under the duvet without disturbing Natasha, but at the sign of movement, she woke up.

"Where are you going?" she asked sleepily.

"I've got to sign on," he whispered.

Natasha yawned and stretched herself awake. "I'll come with you."

"What for?"

"I want to. I might help you find a job," she smiled.

Marcus was still amazed at how chirpy she could be when she woke.

"You don't have to, you can stay in bed. I won't be long," Marcus said as he switched on the kettle then walked to the bathroom.

Natasha got out of bed, pulled on her knickers and a T-shirt, went to the cupboard, took out two mugs and put a spoonful of coffee in each. She measured three spoonfuls of sugar into Marcus' mug.

"Do you want toast?" she hollered over the sound of Marcus' peeing.

"Yes please."

She found the loaf of bread and made a plateful of toast, filled the cups with hot water as the kettle boiled and took a drink from one. Marcus returned from the bathroom and took a slice of toast.

"Is the water hot?" Natasha asked, handing him his mug.

"Yes."

"Right, I'll have a shower before we go."

Claudia came out of the Superintendent's office and walked along the corridor to the canteen. She saw Taff and Stephanie at a table eating bacon sandwiches with their cups of tea and signalled for them to join her. She waited for the pair to gulp down their tea and pick up their sarnies.

"I've just come from the Super's," Claudia said, taking a seat behind her desk. "We're running out of time. He's stood down the rest of the squad and unless we come up with something solid fast - then we're history."

Claudia waited until the two detectives finished their sandwiches before getting up and walking to a marker board. She drew a line dividing the board into two and wrote Andrea and Michelle at the head of each column.

"Right, let's go over this slowly and see if we've missed anything glaringly obvious. Let's start with Andrea. Everybody who is involved in this case we know about that *could* have done it."

Taff picked a piece of bacon from his teeth, wiped his hand on a tissue. "Her grandfather and her uncle."

Claudia began writing on the board as the names were shouted out.

"Lydia," Stephanie suggested.

"Her father."

"A client or a stranger."

"A gay lover."

"One of her uncle's 'associates'," Taff added.

"Anyone else you can think of?" Claudia asked when the two detectives fell silent.

"That's about it," said Taff.

"Okay, we can eliminate Lydia, her grandfather, her uncle and her father," said Claudia, crossing them from the board as she spoke.

"We know that two of the people connected and charged with her uncle are still inside. The officers that handled the case are convinced that there were others involved. They stripped down and thoroughly examined Piers Bailey's computers but couldn't prove any links to him. It would take us forever to investigate every paedophile; even if we had the resources," Taff stated.

Claudia nodded her head. "I agree. Now Michelle."

They went through the process again.

"Have all the girls at the club been checked out? We haven't missed any?"

"None guv, they were *all* interviewed and looked into," said Stephanie.

Claudia looked up to the board. "So that leaves only, a client, a gay lover, one of Bailey's friends or a stranger, agreed?"

Both the detectives nodded in agreement.

"We've spoken to all the clients that showed up on her phone; and we've confirmed that she had no other registered phone."

"Unless she had another one of those pay as you go jobs," suggested Claudia.

"Which we can assume she didn't; otherwise we would have found it; unless the killer took it, in which case we're hardly likely to find it," Taff said. "It doesn't help that she worked from home. Any one of her tricks could have told a friend, who mentioned it to a friend who just happened to be in town."

"As for the gay lover angle – we've been in touch with the gay community groups - nada. No former lover has come forward," said Stephanie.

"That leaves only a stranger, which we all agree that without some stroke of luck is going to be bloody hard to find."

Claudia walked back to her desk and sat back down. "Is this about the girls' lifestyle? There haven't been any other similar cases; so is it personal? Taff what do you think?"

"I think the favourite's got to be a client."

"Stephanie?"

"They let the killer in; it's either a client or a casual pick up."

Claudia nodded. "Right, Taff I know we've done this before, but I want you to go over her clients again. Stephanie you take the gay bars and clubs."

Darren stepped off the train and walked to the entrance of Eltham station. She kept him waiting of course; shifting from foot to foot trying to take a big interest in the betting shop window. A slight figure swamped in a puffy jacket, with skinny legs below came into view. For a split second he failed to recognize her; thought it was some street kid coming up with the traditional demand: "'Scuse me, have you got a spare cigarette?"

"Hey!" Jojo, who sometimes watched American TV shows with her mother, called out.

"Hello babes," muttered Darren, taking her arm as they hustled off towards Mandela Crescent.

As on his previous visit, Darren was struck by how nice the house was, really. In spite of all the shit that went down over this way, the houses were modern and tasteful, honey-coloured brick with green roof tiles, a sort of mini-Docklands in style. Recent rebuilds, after the old terraces had been demolished, finishing the work begun by the Luftwaffe in the Second World War. Darren and Jojo did not know this as a fact, it was an awareness bred in their bones. They could both have recognized the name "Hitler", but would have had to think to come up with his nationality.

Even before she'd shut the front door, Jojo had shrugged off her jacket and suddenly, the mission was all worthwhile.

She was slim as a pencil, but luscious. Her breasts were ripe, dusky against the white jersey, crammed into a crop-top that showed off the compulsory belly ring. She filled her size eight jeans to perfection, pouting through a sticky mass of fluorescent lip gloss, and wore shiny silver sandals with little kitten heels.

Darren steadied himself on the doorjamb as his feelings for this astonishing creature raised a storm of desire. They had done it once already; quickly, in the park in the old boathouse. So cold to begin with. He remembered the dampness of the bare planks through the back of his tee shirt, and Jojo's little hands sliding up between the cloth and his skin. How his muscles had rippled with pleasure under the feel of it.

Jojo had known about the boathouse, about the padlock that was broken, but which hung misleadingly in place.

"Kids come in here to smoke," she said, "and drink. The ones who can't get in to a pub yet."

"I'm getting splinters!" she'd giggled. Then they had been too busy for giggling, there had been … a starburst and then it was over. Jojo springing up, little shrieks as she pulled her clothes back up, squeals of "Oh my God! What have I done with my shoe? Look at my top!"

Her sophistication confirmed his assessment of her age - eighteen, maybe nineteen. She looked old enough to get served in pubs. Might be quite clever, maybe still at school in the sixth form or at college, although she didn't really come over as studious.

Now, as she had in the park, Jojo put a hand casually up to her dark curls. Silver nails with glue-on extensions, because she had bitten her own down. She wanted people to notice the improvements. Although young, she knew that raising her arm to play with her hair lifted her bosom, while leaning forward deepened her cleavage. She liked people to notice that, too.

Two of the male teachers at school had especially noticed; one of the young ones, Ayo Agade, who taught Maths, and old Mr Jarvis who took her set for History. They both lost the thread when Jojo played her tricks. It was funny. It was fucking hilarious, so long as you could get them on their own. Didn't know what to do with their selves. Then you were really in charge. And they were supposed to be the teachers. If that wasn't funny, what was? Frankly it was pathetic, how easy it was to gain power over people. You couldn't help playing tricks, when it was that laughably easy.

She eyed Darren up and down. He really wasn't bad, not bad at all. Besides the usual equipment of a reasonably good-looking guy, Darren had a sensual turn to his mouth and an edgy but somehow relaxed way of standing or sitting still that gave away the simple fact that he was highly sexed. He knew that: it just embarrassed him. He had yet to grasp how attractive it made him.

The trouble was, Darren hadn't let himself gain the basic experience that would have converted his assets into sheer, joyous pulling power. Since middle school, aged ten, the girls had latched onto his animal magnetism. That was why they had followed him around the playground, taunting and teasing, showing off and sneering, trying to get his attention.

Being a bit of a Mummy's boy Darren had failed to read between the lines. They fancied him. His shyness was an affront, and came over as rejection. Then they'd started calling out that he was a queer, a torment that had continued until his growth spurt at Senior School. All this had put Darren behind in his relations with the opposite sex.

"Come on," she urged.

"What?"

Darren tried to keep the hunger out of his gaze. Jojo who had her hand on the stair post, was turning to urge him on. Her face in three-quarter profile was entrancingly pretty.

"We've got until late. Mum's off out 'til ten or eleven, could even be after that. Let's go to my room, yeah?"

Her room? It was a big bedroom, looking over the back, with tiny gardens (more like patios), and more low-rise housing right down to the river, it seemed. Darren tried to think of a way to describe it, this odd lack of hills and slopes that you saw up the estuary end of London. "Flatlands" he thought. That was about it. There couldn't be two rooms this big upstairs. There was a double bed with a furry animal-print throw over it, and a turquoise silky dressing gown on a hanger behind the door.

"This really yours?" said the dumbfounded Darren. "Where does your Mum sleep, then."

"She has the little room. She likes it. She's afraid of … of open spaces, my mum. You know?"

"My auntie's like that," Darren volunteered. "She had to stop working because she was afraid to go out. But she didn't mind just an ordinary size room."

"Ordinary! That's nice, I must say! I thought you'd like my room," she huffed, arms crossed.

"Yeah I do, it's really nice. I was just thinking it seemed more like someone older's. Some one bigger," he hastily amended, glancing at the turquoise wrap. His mother would kill him, Darren thought, if he took a girl into her room.

"You got a problem?" Jojo demanded, hands behind her back, fiddling crossly with her bra clasp (it was a pretty bra, new from Primark, black and satiny with latticed insets); "because you're supposed to be doing this; you prat."

Darren accepted that *where* was not up for discussion. Whatever was happening was happening here, now, on the exotic fur throw; and who could refuse?

"Sorry," he muttered.

He fumbled with the hooks, noticing as he reached for them the traces of white paint still caught in the skin of his knuckles. They sank back together into the fake fur, mouths clamped; Jojo's lips were sticky, tasting of sugar and strawberries.

Natasha walked to the computer terminal in the Jobcentre while Marcus waited in the queue. She navigated her way through the simple process, following the menu until the machine offered a list of suitable vacancies that matched her selections. She printed off two jobs and waited for Marcus. When he had finished signing, he joined Natasha.

"There's a couple here I think you should go for," she said taking his hand.

"Yes? Let's have a look at them then," Marcus said.

"Well what do you think?"

Marcus finished reading. "Sounds alright; salary's not brilliant though."

Natasha squeezed his hand. "It's better than nothing."

"True. Okay, I'll give it a try. Where's the other one?"

"Here it is," she said showing him another printout.

"This is for an insurance salesman," he said.

"Can't you do that?"

"Course I can, but its commission based. See it says O.T.E." said Marcus pointing at the relevant letters.

"What does that mean?" Natasha asked.

"It means On Target Earnings. That's what you get *if* you reach sales targets; which most people can't. Look at the basic – that's less than a hundred and fifty quid a week."

"Sorry. Well go for the first one."

They walked to a desk where a large white woman dressed in a thick hand knitted cardigan was seated. She peered over the top of her glasses, cursorily inspected Marcus, decided his needs were not as important as her need to use the phone and dismissively showed him to a chair. Marcus waited patiently, whilst the woman arranged her bingo night before replacing the receiver.

"Can I help you?" she asked dubiously.

Marcus handed her the printout. "Can I get the details of this job?"

"Have you got the necessary qualifications?"

"I wouldn't have bothered if I didn't, would I?" Marcus replied sarcastically and felt Natasha's pinch.

The adviser sneered, picked up the phone, dialled the number and had a brief conversation. After a few questions she covered the mouthpiece.

"Can you attend an interview tomorrow?"

Marcus nodded.

The adviser concluded the call and hung up the phone. "You've got to be there at ten thirty. I've written all the details down. Can you manage that?"

"I'm jobless not brainless thank you," Marcus said, then winced as he received another pinch.

"Well I never!" the insulted adviser said with disgust.

"I bet you didn't. Bye."

Marcus smiled. It was worth the pinch.

Taff checked the address on the card then knocked on the door, which was eventually opened by a smartly dressed man in his fifties. When he identified himself, the man walked outside and hastily shut the door.

After ten minutes of tense questioning, Taff was satisfied that he had learned all he could and allowed the nervous, embarrassed man to rejoin his family.

Five down ten to go he thought as he walked to the car and headed for the next address.

Chapter 13

Marcus turned down the gas then neatly emptied the scrambled eggs onto the plate beside the two rashers of bacon, plantain, lightly fried tomatoes and baked beans.

The doorbell rang and Marcus opened the door to Natasha who had copies of newspapers in her arms. She kissed him, followed him inside, then sat on the stool beside him in the kitchen and snagged a piece of the fried plantain that she had been introduced to by Marcus.

"Do you want some breakfast?"

Natasha shook her head. "No. You get yourself ready."

"I've got plenty of time."

"I'll have a cup of coffee then."

"Are you sure you wouldn't like something to eat?"

"Yes."

He poured her a cup of coffee then sat down to his breakfast.

"How are you feeling?"

"Nervous," Marcus said as he cut a piece of bacon and placed it onto his fork.

Natasha stroked his thighs lovingly and took in how good he looked. She cuddled closer towards him, taking in the mixed smell of baby lotion and after-shave. "Relax, you'll be fine."

"I hope you're right."

Claudia sat behind her desk reading files. She picked up one labelled Marcus Carpenter and opened it. She took up her pen to make notes. Something about the man troubled her; but she couldn't put her finger on what. Despite her suspicions, the man had no previous convictions. There were a couple of parking and speeding tickets, but not one criminal offence; certainly nothing of the nature she was thinking of.

Marcus took a seat opposite the female receptionist in the smart office. No expense appeared to have been spared on the lavish fittings. The company logo sat straddled between two gigantic pieces of Modern Art, which Marcus assumed had astronomical financial value.

Steel tastefully interwoven with wood painted in the company's colours emphasized the desired corporate image. If daunting was the effect they were aiming for, then he felt they had succeeded.

Marcus adjusted his tie and pulled at the sleeve of his jacket nervously. It had been a long time since he had worn the suit and hoped it didn't look dated.

He checked his hands to make sure that his nails were clean, then brought them to his freshly shaven face and sniffed the after shave to reassure himself he had not splashed on too much.

The middle-aged receptionist smiled at him as she sorted out the mail, placed them into the relevant pigeonholes and simultaneously, efficiently answered the phone every time she spotted the flashing light.

An auburn haired woman in her late-twenties, wearing a smart business suit emerged from an office and marched up to Marcus, exuding extreme confidence and authority.

"Mr Carpenter?"

Marcus stood up. "Yes."

"Hello. I'm Chloe Thomas," she announced, extending her hand and shaking his with the merest hint of a smile. "Let's go through to my office."

Marcus followed and waited as she walked behind her desk.

"Please take a seat."

"Thank you," Marcus smiled and sat down.

Ms Thomas picked up a copy of his CV and studied it briefly before speaking. She looked up, "Okay Mr Carpenter, tell me about yourself" she said in a professional manner.

"As you can see from CV, I've a lot of experience in an administrative role," Marcus replied confidently.

Natasha switched on the music system and set about reading the newspapers. She had circled two jobs and was considering another when the doorbell rang. She put down the paper, turned down the volume of the music system and opened the door.

"Hello, can I help you?" she asked the black woman.

"Is Mr Carpenter in?"

"No, I'm sorry he isn't."

"Do you know when he'll be back?" the woman asked, obviously disappointed.

"He should be back soon. Would you like to come in and wait?"

"No, I'll come back some other time," the woman smiled. "May I ask, are you his partner?"

"Not exactly."

"I see."

"Are you sure I can't take a message?" Natasha asked.

"There's no need. I'll speak to him some other time," the woman confirmed and before Natasha could ask her name, turned and left.

Natasha closed the door. She turned the music back up. *Was* she his partner she wondered? Nothing had really been said, should she ask Marcus where they were at, and exactly what was her status?

The thing that she really loved about Marcus was his immediate acceptance of her for what she was. They were so alike in many ways. Despite his age, he never tried to make her feel stupid, useless or weak like so many others. He wasn't afraid to let her make decisions; something she had only ever done before for her mother in those dark days. She knew she felt more confident now, thanks to Marcus. She smiled inwardly, partner had sounded right though.

She leapt to her feet and grabbed her jacket, making sure she had the spare key Marcus had given her before shutting the door.

Claudia left Lambton House, got in her car and waited a while. The sight of the young white woman in the flat had thrown her a little. She wondered if her initial instincts had been wrong. She had felt sure that Marcus was a loner. Her mobile rang. She answered it, had a brief conversation then drove off.

Natasha was curled up on the bed watching TV when Marcus entered the bed-sit, still resplendent in his suit.

"How did it go?" Natasha asked excitedly, rushing to smother him in kisses.

"I don't think I'll get it," he said disappointedly.

"Why?"

"She thought the job was not enough of a challenge and that I'd get bored with it."

Natasha wrapped her arms around his waist. "I'm sorry," she consoled.

"Me too, I think she was just fobbing me off."

"Don't let it get to you," she said, planting another kiss on his lips. "You've got to believe in yourself. Don't give up Marcus."

"I know," he smiled half-heartedly.

Natasha pointed to the vase on the table. "I bought some flowers." She led him to the sofa. "I think we should brighten up this flat once you get a job. And you will, trust me. Look, I've marked out some jobs I think you should have a look at," she said cheerily, picking up the papers.

"I'll do that later," he said giving her a peck on the lips, "come on let's go for a drink."

Claudia took her seat in the chair opposite a sombre looking Superintendent Middleton.

"I'm sorry Claudia; I'm taking you off the Bailey case."

"I thought you said I had another week sir?"

"I know what I said, and it's no reflection on you or your team, but let's face it there hasn't been much progress; and I need you on another case. We've got a missing fourteen-year-old girl," Superintendent Middleton explained.

Claudia rested back in her chair, the disappointment lightened slightly. "How long has she been missing?"

"Seventy-two hours."

"Seventy-two hours! When did the parents report her missing?"

"An hour ago; they're still being interviewed."

Claudia sat forward. "What! Why did they wait so long?"

Superintendent Middleton could see the interest in her face. "They thought she was at her father's. The parents are divorced and the girl often spends nights at his place. The mother only realised she was missing when the father phoned."

"It doesn't look good Claudia. As soon as the press gets hold of this, you know how they are going to react. I need someone who can handle the press and protect the parents when they start the circus," he explained.

Claudia clasped her hands behind her head. "What's going to happen to the Bailey case?"

Superintendent Middleton stood up and walked to look out of the window, his back to Claudia. "I'll keep Morgan and Elford on it for a while, but not much longer before it goes into the cold cases."

"If you don't mind sir, I'd like Elford on this one with me."

Superintendent Middleton turned around and raised his eyes in doubt, "Are you sure? She's not very experienced Claudia."

"I'm positive. She's a good copper sir."

"Okay," he accepted. "Come on you'd better meet the parents; hopefully we can find this girl pretty sharpish."

Natasha raised her head from the pillow and reached across Marcus' naked body for the half-smoked spliff.

"I wish I didn't have to go back next week."

Marcus stroked her left breast. "Me too."

"Do you really mean that?"

"Nah," Marcus teased.

Natasha dug him in the ribs and lit the spliff.

"I've been thinking about what you said," whispered Marcus.

Natasha was puzzled. "What did I say?"

"About seeing my son - I think you're right. Fuck Maxine. I want to see him."

"Is that who that woman was?" Natasha asked.

"What woman?"

"Shit. I forgot to tell you. She came round a couple of days ago. The day you went for the interview."

"Maxine? She wouldn't come here. She doesn't even know where I live. What did she look like?"

"I think she was in her thirties. Long hair - it was straightened. She was about five foot eight, well-built and she was wearing a pin striped trouser suit."

Marcus recognised the description. "Oh her, I know her. That's not Maxine."

"Who is she then?"

"She's a policewoman."

"What did she want?"

"I don't know," Marcus lied, "she came here before to ask about that murder."

"Well she said she'd be back," Natasha said passing him the spliff. "What are you going to do about your son?"

"I'm going to speak to a solicitor."

"Do you realise you never call him by his name," Natasha said resting her head on his chest.

Marcus dragged hard on the spliff, "It's Monju."

Natasha raised her head and looked at him. "What?"

"Don't look at me," Marcus said. "She chose it."

"Well it's original!" After a brief pause she added, "What's he like?"

"He's cheeky, clever and just loveable - my little man," Marcus said emotively.

He reached into the drawer, took out the photo from the bedside cabinet and passed it to Natasha.

"Oh Marcus, he's gorgeous!" she squealed.

"I know. Do you know for ages after Maxine kicked me out I couldn't bear to look at children in the street. It would only take the sight of a child around Monju's age with their parent and I would start crying. I felt so jealous of them and yet I just didn't know what to do. I can't tell you how much I hated Meryl Streep for taking that role in 'Kramer versus Kramer'."

Marcus pulled on the spliff and passed it back to Natasha. "When he was born I don't think I could have been happier. I just loved him from day one and didn't want him to go through the experiences I had."

He took a deep breath.

"You see my parents had me late in their lives. My mother was fifty-one and my father fifty-six. She didn't even know that she was pregnant until her fifth month. I don't know if she'd have kept me if she had known earlier - probably not," he said, sucking in more air.

"From very early on they let me know that I was an accident, that I had come along at the wrong time and upset all their plans. They made me feel like an unwanted gift that they had to keep. As soon as I was legally responsible for myself, they were up and off back to Antigua. I was determined not to let my son feel the way I did."

132

"When I was growing up, it was as though they were ashamed of me. I was never allowed to have friends come the house; not that I had many friends - they saw to that. What with belonging to the Church, I was expected to come home straight from school. That was it; my life consisted of Church and home. Not knowing anything else, I made myself believe that they acted like this because I was special and they really cared."

Natasha stubbed out the butt. "Don't you have any other family?

"I've got a brother Courtney; but I don't *know* him. He was twenty-three years old by the time I was born. Their *real* son. He left to go to college in the States when I was two, before my parents joined the Church. He's an attorney over there now. He was lucky I guess; he escaped the Church. I can count on the fingers of one hand how many times I've seen him. At first we exchanged cards, always signed with the same message – 'All the best', never 'With Love' or anything sentimental. Eventually the cards became less frequent until they finally stopped."

Natasha lowered her lips to his and kissed him. "You've got to see your son Marcus. He's going to need to know that you still love him."

Chapter 14

Claudia replaced the phone. "Stephanie I want you to go to the Mason's. Ring me when you get there."

"Right guv," Stephanie said, reaching for her bag.

"The press conference is arranged for twelve, so make sure that you're ready for the onslaught," Claudia added as Stephanie started for the door.

Natasha looked up from the paper, "Are you any good with computers?" she asked.

"Pretty good. I'm not a dinosaur you know."

She poked out her tongue at him, "Just asking; besides you haven't got one. How about this?"

She showed him an advert for a computer software installer that she had spotted.

Marcus read the ad. "I don't know that much, not to install them I mean."

"It says training with guaranteed employment on completion of the course."

"Hmmm," Marcus said sceptically.

"Well at least give them a ring. You never know," Natasha said, tossing him her mobile phone.

Marcus rang the number and had to endure the torrent of kisses from Natasha when he was invited for an interview.

Taff was quite surprised when he entered the pub. Even taking into account the fact that it was a mid-week afternoon, the place was hardly busy. He wondered if the place had been going long? It certainly couldn't pay the exorbitant rent bills the area commanded based on this number of clients.

The few customers present were all women (surprise, surprise). A suited couple sat at a table eating a meal, occasionally openly exchanging kisses and swapping furtive touches. Three other tables were in use and the remaining four customers sat beside the bar.

Taff approached the butch looking woman behind the bar, grateful that neither of his daughters had stupidly adorned their noses, eyes or lips with piercings such as hers. Surely five metal spikes in your face was unnecessary?

Couldn't say anything nowadays though could you? Dare to express an opinion and you would be branded sexist. These days you had to respect every form of sexuality even if you thought it sordid or offensive. God knows how he would react should either Serena or Laura turn up with a girl like this barmaid. He shuddered at the thought.

Taff caught himself and remembered the words of Andrea's grandfather. He had found the man so loathsome and yet here he was expressing thoughts others might interpret as being equally offensive. He shook his head. One day he would get the hang of this Political Correctness stuff.

He took out the two photographs. "Do you recognise either of these two ladies," he asked handing across the photos.

The barmaid took a while to study the pictures, fiddling annoyingly with her nose ring, before answering. "Definitely not, sorry; pity I like the look of the black girl," she winked and handed back the pictures.

"Oh well. Thanks for your time," Taff said, slipping the photos back into the envelope as he turned to leave. Please God never let my girls turn out like this he prayed. Also, fuck PC! Only twenty more knocks he thought.

Marcus sat opposite the portly middle-aged, ruddy-faced man, sensing that the interview had gone well. The man stood up and smiled as he shook Marcus' hand.

"Congratulations Marcus. I can tell you here and now you've been accepted on the course."

Marcus got off the bus, still in the suit he had worn to the interview. He walked up the car park stairs, checked around, making sure no one was lurking around unseen watching , then bent down removed the loose bricks to retrieve his stash and left casually.

135

Stephanie fetched three cups of tea then joined Claudia and Katherine Mason in the living room.

The three women sat in the cramped living room.

A tabby cat marched purposefully across the room to brush against Stephanie's leg; fearlessly demanding attention. It was immediately rewarded as Stephanie reached down lazily to gently stroke his back. The cat raised its tail in appreciation.

"Mrs Mason, what time exactly did you last see Jodie?"

"It was just before I went to work on Thursday. I work part-time at Sainsbury's." Katherine, picked up the packet, flicked it open, dangled a cigarette between her lips and lit it in one smooth action. She blew out a cloud of smoke before continuing, "My car is in the garage and I need the extra money to get it repaired, so now that Jodie's old enough to take care of herself, I do the night shift," she explained. "And please call me Kath everyone does."

She dragged on the cigarette again, "The bus stop's just round the corner, not five minutes away, so I left at seven to catch the ten past."

"Has Jodie ever gone missing before Kath?"

"No, not this long."

"So she has?"

Katherine Mason crossed her legs and brushed the fringe from her eyes. "Well she's stayed out with friends before and not phoned to tell me, but she's normally back the next day or phoned to say where she is."

"Have you any ideas where she could be?"

"I've phoned all her friends I know."

"Did she say if she was going out that night? Claudia asked.

Katherine Mason shook her head, "No."

"How did you two get on?"

Katherine gave Claudia a suspicious look. "We were close. She wouldn't have run away if that's what you're trying to get at."

"That's not what I meant Katherine. I just want you to be aware that we might find out things about her she kept from you. Things about her you didn't know. I want you to be prepared."

"Kath, not Katherine, only my parents call me Katherine."

"Sorry Kath. I was trying to ask whether she had any problems she may have kept from you."

"She's a teenager. She's going through adolescence. Everything's a problem, but she would have told me if she had something on her mind. We didn't keep secrets."

"Kath, do you have a picture of Jodie that we can have?"

Katherine unfurled her long legs and walked to a tallboy, rummaged around and returned with a 7x5 inch photo, "this is a recent one," she said, handing it to Claudia.

The girl in the picture did not look like a young teenager. Despite being only around five foot four, Jodie's long black hair, dusky skin colouring and already generous breasts gave the impression of a much older young woman. Claudia's mind tried to blot out the images of the young Jodie crying, pleading as someone as plausible yet as repulsive as Piers Bailey violated her.

"She gets her colouring from her father, he's Turkish," Kath explained.

"Did she have a boyfriend?" Claudia asked.

"I think she broke up with her last bloke about four weeks ago. She hadn't brought anyone new home, so I guess not."

"You mean you let a fourteen-year-old have boyfriends stay the night!" Claudia caught herself and instantly rued her words. Where had that come from?

Katherine looked across at Claudia and caught her disapproving look. "Don't judge me. I'm a good mother. I was sixteen when I had Jodie," she said stubbing out the cigarette and pointing to the image in the photo. "As you can see, Jodie is an attractive girl. She has had boys running after her since she was twelve. When she told me that she wasn't a virgin, I decided it was best that if she was having sex, then at least she should be safe. I don't want her to do something stupid like I did that might affect her life, so I allowed her to bring boyfriends home." She opened the packet and lit another cigarette. "I gave her space, I'm sure that she hasn't run away. She had no reason to."

Claudia felt a rush of guilt. Here she was judging this woman, doubting what kind of mother she was (or had been God forbid) – making assumptions that the fact that her daughter had gone missing was a reflection on her parenting skills.

How was she going to deal with motherhood and bringing up a child herself? What if *her* child turned out bad? Face it she thought, he or she would be burdened by being the offspring of a police officer; would be under great pressure from other children.

"Have you got a school photo? One of her in her uniform, we might get better results – people will sympathise more if they imagine her as young and vulnerable," Claudia said in her most caring voice.

The cat leapt up and made himself comfortable on Stephanie's lap, twitching his ears contentedly. As she got up to fetch another photo, Katherine blew out a wisp of smoke that drifted towards Stephanie, who wondered if smokers were deliberately targeting her for persecution. Maybe she could get away for a few moments to chant.

Marcus joined the long line of travellers leaving Lewisham Station and walked for ten minutes through the centre of town, which soon turned into leafy suburbia, then over the common and into Greenwich Park. Once inside, he sat down on the damp grass and waited for Natasha under a big, big tree. He had guessed her route and worked out that she would come along in the next ten minutes or so. He hadn't seen her running yet. He could have simply arranged to meet her there, but wanted to watch her without her knowing that she was being observed.

It would be like re-living that first moment when he had really noticed her. Then all she had been was that nice but nondescript young woman from his flats who lived away most of the time; whom he had unexpectedly seen from his window (only weeks ago!) toiling up the road, so burdened with baggage that she could hardly make her way.

It was past 11 o'clock now and the sun was up. Marcus lay back and basked, shading his eyes in the unreliable Spring warmth. He watched the path, already busy with family outings, dog walkers, sunbathers and a smattering of tourists, all enjoying Sunday. Looking at handsome houses, fine landscapes and the view over an awesome palace, Marcus had been close to forgetting about beautiful things. Could you imagine that – enjoying Sunday?

He recalled how hiis own childhood Sundays had been dreary beyond belief. The Church of the Final Coming had seen to that. Not content with spoiling his week, the Reverend Mackenzie had ensured that Marcus' one homework-free, errand-free day had been a masochistic celebration of dullness and bad food. His mother would put it all in a slow oven before services began at 10.00 a.m., so that dinner was dried out by the time they ate at 2.45 p.m., allowing just enough time for digestion before evening prayers began at 6.00 p.m. There wasn't even any real music or singing. The Reverend's henchman would intone some bitter line from some grim prophecy and the rest of them would chant it afterwards.

Marcus knew other pupils at his school that came from churchgoing families, but their Sundays entailed floral frocks and best shirts. Mothers wore fancy hats; there was singing, gossip and ample flirting. Sure the kids grumbled, but until they transformed into rebellious teens, the truth was, that they enjoyed it.

The 'Final Comers' were committed to sobriety of attire. They believed the Reverend Mackenzie when he reminded them endlessly, that joy was totally out of place with the end of the world and the Last Judgement close at hand. Austerity and modesty could have been their motto.

Marcus wondered why his parents had fallen for it? They hadn't always worn dowdy clothes, pursed up their mouths, or walked as if their bodies were made of lead and only their legs were flesh and blood when they moved – not if Marcus could believe the Griffiths'. His former neighbours had talked to him when he was only a teenager, after his parents left to go back to Antigua where they could spread the words of the Church. The Griffiths' had always worried about him. Now he began to hear about his family history at suppers they invited him to, because they doubted he could cook for himself.

He had learnt that until his brother Courtney left home, all had been well. His mother and father had been god-fearing, but normal. When her beloved only child headed for the States to seek his fortune, Philomena had fallen victim to what Mrs Griffiths had called 'Empty Nest' depression. What had tipped them though was the incident when his father, Alton, had been accused of sexually harassing a female colleague. The fact that he had been cleared when the woman (a conductress with a penchant for black men) he had only worked with for a week when his regular partner had been ill, confessed to making up the story to hide her cheating on her boyfriend; had provided them little solace. The damage had been done.

Somehow, Marcus was conceived in this dark time. It was during his mother's pregnancy, that she along with a friend from their regular Baptist Church switched allegiance to the Church of the

Final Coming. (The Reverend Mackenzie was a fine looking man in those days.) His father followed suit, and was soon even more zealous than his wife. Having experienced corruption first hand, Alton felt this austere religion would get the smell out of his nostrils.

By the time Marcus was born, the family were so thoroughly sucked in to the cult – both socially and financially - that even the Griffiths' next door were kept at arm's length. Soon there was no more shared tea drinking or Bank Holiday outings.

Even the Griffiths' youngest daughter, Sharon, whose cheerful personality enhanced her plainness and almost made her seem beautiful, was gravely turned away when she called to ask if she could take the baby Marcus to the local park.

An errant football rolled past Marcus, closely followed by an excited youth, shouting loudly in anguish as he recovered the wayward pass.

For Marcus, the park was a short cut that he was only allowed to hurry through on his way home from school or the shops. He was trained up the way he should go; focused on chores and respect for his elders. His parents were genuinely older than most, but they behaved like old, old people. If he stayed at school for football practice, he condemned them to some source of dangerous exertion, like watering the vegetable patch or going all the way to the corner Chemist themselves, or having to get his tea late instead of reading a chapter of Revelation.

On one unforgettable occasion, he had lingered in the park to play cricket with other ten year olds. Having forgotten the time in his enjoyment, Marcus was late home by an hour. At last, as he hurried up their front path, warm and full of life, the door slowly opened before him to reveal his father, shirt loose over his uniform trousers with his hands on his chest, gasping.

Marcus had been supposed to rush a prescription to the corner Pharmacy that afternoon, to collect a fresh asthma inhaler, just in case his father had one of his attacks. His mother had gone for the medication herself. When Marcus got home, guilty and miserable, she was sitting heavily at the kitchen table, shaking her head slowly, getting over the walk.

No one scolded him, but that Sunday the main sermon (for there were several) had made pointed references to "those who lingered in the glades of pleasure, while the jaws of hell gaped w- i-i-i--ide before them." From that day on, Marcus became more unconvinced of the Reverend and The Church.

Natasha slowed to a walk and checked her watch before she began the steep stroll up the steps to Greenwich Park, which served as her warm down. Not bad, her times were getting better and she wasn't even conscious of the looks she received from those around her any more. In fact she was so focused she did not become aware of Marcus until he rose from his prone position on the grass and shouted her name.

She smiled as he joined her on the path and started walking beside her.

"You spoiled my surprise."

"Pardon?"

"I wanted to see how your running was coming along, and then maybe invite you to mine for a meal," Marcus explained.

"So are you withdrawing the invitation then?"

"Of course not, but I don't think you deserve dessert."

"Well in that case I shan't bring any wine or the movie," said Natasha, poking her tongue out playfully.

They walked back across Blackheath common to Lambton House.

"Give me time to shower and get changed and I'll be round," Natasha said, kissing him goodbye as they entered the block.

On a high, Marcus closed the door to his bed-sit, made his way to the kitchen and opened cupboards that were full of items he had purchased in Lewisham the day before with some of the notes from one of the jiffy envelopes. This was proper stuff; not the usual cheap, mundane compromises he had grown accustomed to of late.

He took the four chicken breasts from the fridge, washed his hands and began skinning them.

Next, he scooped some butter and placed it in a glass bowl, chopped some of the fresh parsley, chives and garlic he had bought from the market, sprinkled some salt and pepper then blended the whole mixture and placed the bowl in the fridge to chill.

Forty minutes later, Marcus returned to the kitchen, opened the oven door, removed the foil from over the tray of chicken breasts, and set the timer for a further fifteen minutes.

141

He washed and placed some broccoli in a pan of salted boiling water, melted some butter in another pan and made a cheese sauce, which he poured on top of the now softened broccoli and placed it in the oven to join the Kievs.

"I can't believe how quickly the past five weeks have gone," Natasha said happily, her mood heightened by the effects of the delicious meal Marcus had cooked, the brandy they had washed it down with and the subsequent lovemaking.

"Me neither," replied Marcus.

"You won't mind if I ring, will you?" she asked.

"Of course not."

"It's just that so much has happened, hasn't it?"

"You can say that again."

"And you can always phone me if you need to or want to," she added hopefully.

"I know Natasha."

"I'm sorry. I sound like a silly teenager don't I?"

Marcus kissed her, "No. It's nice to know someone cares."

"I just want you to know I love you."

"You don't have to say anything."

"I know, but I want to," she kissed him, lay her head on his chest and sniffed, "I'm going to miss your smell."

"Hey I wash every day."

"No. You know what I mean," she said looking into his eyes. "I won't be unfaithful. I promise you."

Marcus held a finger to her lips. "Shh. Don't." He looked at his watch. "Come on, you've got to finish packing."

Natasha bit his shoulder playfully and started stroking his cock, only to receive a smack on her bum.

"Out of my bed you wicked woman!"

"Killjoy!" she said.

The large crowd streamed out of the cinema. Laura Morgan linked her arm into her dad's and turned to him. "That was excellent wasn't it?"

Taff looked skywards, "A bit far fetched. I'm sure somewhere out there, there is a place where cars constantly hurtle along at high speeds and no-one gets run over...."

"Don't start dad. It's only a film remember?" Laura said in typical teenage manner.

"Well next time I get to choose, okay?"

Laura groaned. "So long as it's not some boring old black and white film from the dark ages."

"Would I?" Taff smiled. "Shall we get something to eat before I drop you home?"

"Let's go for a drink," Laura suggested.

Taff frowned. "I'm not sure your mother would approve of that."

"Don't be silly dad. I'm not a little girl anymore. I'm nineteen! Mum knows I drink. Come on," she pleaded.

"Alright. If you're sure," Taff conceded. The prospect of a pint after watching such dross seemed a good idea.

"How much longer are you going to be in there Claudia? Ken called out.

Claudia opened her eyes and looked at the pregnancy kit one last time. It was definitely positive. That was all she needed.

"Just coming," she called wearily. She gathered up the kit and put the contents in the pocket of her kimono before opening the door of the en-suite bathroom.

Marcus and Natasha waited patiently at Victoria coach station, hugging each other while the other passengers boarded the coach.

Marcus reached into his pocket. "Don't open it until you get on," he said, handing Natasha a small package.

She took the gift, "you shouldn't have."

"Think of it as a thank you present."

"You didn't have to. Now you've made me feel guilty for not getting you something."

"It's the least I can do after all you've done for me. You've given me my life back" Marcus said and kissed her forehead.

"What is it?" Natasha asked curiously and moved to open the parcel, but Marcus held her hand to prevent her from doing so.

"No; you'll find out when you get on," he chastised.

The coach driver revved up the engine.

Natasha kissed him. "I'll ring you tonight."

"Okay."

"Good luck on the course," she wished, giving him a final kiss before she boarded the coach, walked down the aisle and sat in a window seat.

Marcus waved as the coach pulled off and watched as she waved back. He remained watching as she settled in the seat, her eyes lighting up in delight as she opened the package and saw the platinum thumb ring that was in the box.

Chapter 15

The group of seven women and three men sat expectantly behind tables in the large training room. A male tutor in his forties, stood in front of the group beside a marker board.

"Good morning. My name is Peter Pearson and I'll be your tutor for the next three weeks. You'll probably get sick of the sight and sound of me, but I am here to help. If you need anything or want any assistance at all, don't hesitate to ask.

I know you're all probably a bit nervous today, it's only natural. Don't worry it only gets better." He paused to look around the room and saw the fear and trepidation on the faces.

"Okay I think we should find out a bit about each other, so if we go around the room clockwise and you can all introduce yourself. I just want a couple of sentences - your name and a hobby or something. Okay?"

He was met by a muted response. It was always like this on the first day he thought, lack of confidence, unfamiliarity and tension. Give them a week and he wouldn't be able to stop their interruptions.

He pointed to a redheaded young woman. "Would you like to start?"

The girl blushed, "Hello, my name is Olivia. I'm twenty-three and I like Salsa."

Claudia and Stephanie stepped from the unmarked car and walked towards the gang of youths that were hanging around outside the off-licence in Eltham.

"Five-oh," someone shouted and was greeted with derisive laughter.

"We're looking for Cassandra Winterton," Claudia said in a friendly voice.

A slim figure stepped out of the pack and flicked a cigarette from thin fingers; sex undeterminable under a grey hood, tracksuit bottoms worn low slung to reveal a second pair underneath. The adolescent stopped a matter of feet from the two policewomen and removed the hooded top to reveal a young teenage girl, her face strikingly pretty despite the slight traces of acne.

"I ain't talking to feds!" she said defiantly, looking over her shoulder to make sure that the rest of the 'crew' had witnessed her bravado. "I'm not a grass."

"Cassie, we're looking for Jodie. Her mother says you were her best friend." Stephanie stated, remembering how Kath Mason had insisted on being addressed.

The girl's face dropped and all pretence of toughness receded. She took her hands out of her pocket and led the two police officers around the corner, away from the noisy gang.

"Have you heard from her?" Claudia asked when they were a sufficient distance away from the main pack.

"No."

"Do you know where she could be?"

Cassie shook her head, "I don't know. I've tried phoning and texting, but her number is dead," she brought her fingers to her mouth at her gaffe.

"Was anything bothering her? Do you think she ran away?"

"No. Jodie wouldn't do that."

"Was she seeing anyone? Did she have a boyfriend?

The young girl look worried.

"If you know anything Cassie it's best to tell us so that we can find her."

"Well, she said she was seeing some boy, but he wasn't from round here and she didn't want people to know. She said he was older than her and she didn't want to get him in trouble."

"Did she tell you what his name was?"

"Yes, I think it was Aaron, Warren, Darren or something like that."

"Do you know how old he is?" asked Claudia.

"I don't know, she wouldn't say." She discharged a stream of spit ungraciously on the pavement – immediately regretting her action when she received an icy stare from the black policewoman.

"How long had she been seeing him Cassie?"

"Not long, a couple of weeks or so."

"You said he wasn't from round here, do you know where he's from?"

"No."

146

"Did she tell you how she met him?"

"At a pub in Blackheath," Cassie answered.

"Do you know the name of the pub Cassie?"

The young girl looked up, "Yeah. The *Market Tavern*."

Claudia opened her mouth to ask another question when her phone rang. Stephanie knew something was seriously wrong as she watched the colour drain from her boss's face. She put her arms around Cassie and discreetly led her away.

"Look here's my card. If you think of anything, I mean anything that can help, call me."

Taff switched off the TV, returned to his seat and picked up the glass of whisky. Memories ran through his head. If only he could have his time again, not to be reincarnated in another time; just to go back and put right the wrongs. He had been fortunate to have lived through the times he had; no he wouldn't change that. However, just like everybody, he had made stupid mistakes - mistakes such as cheating on his wife. Not once or twice: Megan might have forgiven him that, but when she had discovered the scale of his infidelity, that had been the final straw.

The divorce hadn't been messy, they had been civil towards each other and Taff had continued seeing the girls. But when Megan had found another man and then subsequently remarried, the result had been less and less contact (and influence) with his daughters. He emptied the glass of its contents.

Claudia and Stephanie walked to the busy scene of crime where uniformed officers were protecting a sealed off area. A Sergeant approached the two women. "Sergeant Shah," he announced and led the way deep into the thick copse, finally stopping at the twisted, gruesome sight of the remains of a young girl that caused Stephanie to throw up.

"Holy shit!" exclaimed Claudia.

Marcus took a swig from the can of beer, his gaze transfixed on the news reporter who was interviewing DI St Clair on TV. As she appealed for witness to the rape and murder of a teenage girl, Marcus wondered if she was working on both cases now.

Without taking his eyes from the screen, he picked up the ringing phone and brought it to his ear.

"Hello."

Natasha's voice sounded, "Hi, it's me."

A picture of the missing young girl looking demure and proper, without any trace of make up, dressed in green and white checked uniform aged around fifteen flashed across the screen. Marcus aimed the remote at the TV and turned down the volume.

"How are you?"

"Alright. Missing you."

"Naturally."

"So tell me about your day," Natasha asked excitedly.

On screen, the reporter thanked the Detective and the news moved on to a different topic, allowing Marcus to focus on his conversation. He turned off the TV and flopped onto the bed. "It was okay. We didn't really do much today."

"How many women on the course?"

Marcus counted each mentally before saying "Seven."

"Seven! Any pretty ones?"

"I honestly didn't really notice."

"Yeah right. Thank God I'm coming down this weekend. I'll remind you of what you're missing," Natasha said, glad that those extra shifts would pay her fare home.

They spoke for another ten minutes, mainly about what the course consisted of and how much they missed each other before they said their goodnights and hung up.

Marcus silently watched his fellow trainees who were grouped together, happily chatting amongst themselves. They were a diverse bunch, and already various friendships and sub-groups were forming.

Although he hadn't really wanted to go along, as it was a celebratory drink marking the end of the first week; it would have been rude not to join them. In the background, *Before Today* by Everything But The Girl blared out from the jukebox.

The redheaded Olivia had managed to position herself beside him and was already drinking her second Red Bull and vodka.

"Are you always this quiet Marcus?" she asked.

"It depends."

"They say it's the quiet ones you have to watch out for," she said licking her lips flirtatiously.

"You don't have to worry about me," Marcus said.

"What do you think of the course?"

"It's okay."

"Yes. I'm enjoying it." She looked straight in his eyes. "Are you single?"

"Sort of."

"Sort of, what does that mean? Are you involved with anyone?"

"Yes. I suppose you could say so," Marcus chuckled.

"You don't seem very sure. How long have you been together?"

"A few weeks."

Olivia raised her eyebrows, "Not that long."

"I suppose not."

"What does she do?"

"She's at university."

Again Olivia raised an eyebrow. "How old is she?"

"Twenty-three."

Olivia smiled, "Same age as me. Where's she studying?"

"Nottingham."

"Do you live alone?"

"Yes."

"So what are you saying?"

Marcus smiled, "Sorry I'm a bit old fashioned."

"Pity," Olivia said disappointedly.

Claudia reached for the knife and set to work about thinly peeling the batch of potatoes. Her mother Naomi, belying her large frame, nimbly crossed the kitchen floor and started to make the large chicken ready for the oven. She sprinkled the bird with chicken seasoning and other herbs while she sang aloud to the Jim Reeves record that her husband Wilbert was playing in the living room of the three-bed-roomed semi where Claudia had grown up.

Claudia finished peeling the last of the potatoes then began dicing some into small pieces for the potato salad that always accompanied the green salad and coleslaw during the Sunday lunch. Claudia enjoyed the comforting, therapeutic ritual.

She moved aside as her mother effortlessly lifted the foil wrapped chicken and placed it in the oven.

"Mum I've got something to tell you," Claudia said apprehensively as she picked up a carrot and began scraping.

Naomi Palmer walked to the fridge and fetched a leg of lamb to the work surface. "What is it darling?" she asked as she transferred the joint to a baking tin.

Claudia bit her lip. "I'm pregnant mum."

"Are you sure?"

Claudia tossed the carrot into a bowl of water and picked up another. "Yes."

Her mother looked at her. "You don't sound too happy about it."

"You know how much Ken and I wanted a family."

Naomi noted the use of the past tense. "I hear a 'but' coming."

"It's not the right time mum."

"What? Claudia tell me when **is** the right time?"

"I don't know. Five years ago or in five years time I suppose."

Naomi heaved, "I take it Ken doesn't know."

"No. I've got to work out what to do first. What's best."

Naomi kissed her teeth. "There's no working out to be done. You've been waiting for this child for how long now? And I don't like to say this, but you are not getting any younger girl."

"You don't have to tell me mum."

Naomi took the knife from her daughter and held her hand, "Sit down."

Both women sat on stools. Naomi reached over and enveloped her daughter in her huge comforting arms. She stroked her daughter's face as though she was still a child.

"Alright. Now tell me what this is all about. What's really bothering you? Are you and Ken having problems?"

Claudia shook her head. "No. Not really. I suppose it's the case that I'm working on; that's part of it. Then there's you and dad."

The older woman was taken aback. "I beg your pardon. What have we got to do with this?"

"Mum, you and dad did without so much to put me through school and university. I know how hard you both worked and I really appreciate it; you know that. I'm so grateful to you."

"Listen Claudia..."

"Please mum let me finish. Thanks to you I've done something with my life that I'm proud of. I've suffered and risen above all the racism and sexism because I knew I wasn't doing this just for me, but for you and dad; for every woman and black person that didn't have the opportunities that you gave me."

Naomi stroked her daughter's hand, "Darling listen to me. Your father and I never went through what we did to make you feel obligated to us. We did it to give you the best we could. We want you to have a better life than we had; but the most important thing we want is for you to be happy."

"And I am mum. That's just it. I love my job and I'm good at it. I *am* doing something positive, something worthwhile that makes a difference to people's lives. I don't know if I can give it up."

Naomi shook her head sadly, "Claudia, I can't tell you what to do. You must talk to Ken and tell him how you feel. You have to search your heart Claudia. Let the Lord guide you."

Later that evening Naomi searched her own heart. Was Claudia suffering from the weight of ambition, and was that her and Wilbert's fault? Perhaps having had only the one child, they had pinned all *their* ambitions on her.

Naomi and Wilbert had been fully aware of their own potential. They believed they had achieved all that had been possible in their generation. Maybe in bringing up this capable child, they had put her under silent pressure - not merely to become a professional, but a high-ranking one.

She conjured up a picture of Claudia, aged eleven, at the big oak dining room table with her homework, steadily shifting her own pile of assignments while the younger kids that Naomi minded settled to their own little bits of homework. Claudia had them organized. A bit of Maths explanation here; ("See these walnuts? Now how many little groups of three can you make from these twelve nuts?"). Some historical insight there - "The ancient Egyptians were a very civilised people...."

151

Claudia had been more than just *clever.* Naomi had glowed with carefully silent pride.

"That's enough of bossing, Claudia," Naomi would tactfully say, when other parents were around. "Richie's intelligent enough to work it out for himself."

If a good woman could bring herself to make the ultimate sacrifice - going without children - for status, then she must not judge her. "But nothing will stop me from grieving," she thought, pulling off her black velvet slippers and easing herself into bed beside Wilbert, who was already asleep.

Marcus waited expectantly at the station as a coach pulled in. He smiled as Natasha got off, ran to him then leapt into his arms and kissed him unashamedly.

Natasha looked on as Marcus jumped from the bed and walked to the neglected pile of records, selected an album, blew off the dust and placed it on the deck of the music system. "Listen to this," he beamed as he ran back naked to join Natasha on the bed, just in time for the track to start. He enveloped Natasha's naked torso in his arms.

"Who is it she asked?"

Marcus smiled. "This is Walter Jackson."

"Any relation to Michael Jackson?"

Marcus shook his head as he listened pensively to the song for a while, comforted by her warmth. Natasha kissed him softly as Walter sang *Tell Me Where It Hurts.*

"Marcus this is beautiful," she cooed.

Marcus accepted her kisses. "He contracted polio when he was seven; can you believe that? Yet if you listen to his voice, you wouldn't know what he had been through. He died of a brain haemorrhage in his forties."

Natasha nestled closer to him as he rejoined her under the covers. His skin was warm and smooth. At first, he was lazy in his lovemaking; she was the one putting in the effort. Then – it was as if she had woken his flesh. He roused, half-rolled over her, and totally took charge.

The weekend was lost in shopping, dancing and making love. On Saturday, they went out together to Habitat and bought things for Marcus' place, picking out tableware and cutlery that was utterly suited for a no-nonsense man. Natasha sought out a large mirror (something she had noticed was conspicuous in its absence from the bed-sit), which she felt would be perfect in his bedroom.

As they wandered around, Marcus remembered the gadgets he had gathered from the same store during his marriage. Then he succeeded in forgetting. They bought black towels for the bathroom, stainless steel stick-on hooks and a filleting knife.

On a roll of euphoria, Natasha led Marcus to browse in *The Pier*, where she persuaded him to buy silly pretty things made of gilt mesh and glass beads; an embroidered table runner, a plain carved wooden bird and a great bottle of scented oil that you could dip tapers in to scent the room.

They went drinking, and were told about a club in the town centre where the music was good and they could dance until very, very late. So they did. The gay barman took a shine to Marcus. When he gave them their drinks he looked daggers at Natasha, and tossed his ponytail, which made her almost hysterical, because Marcus hadn't noticed.

She was sobbing with silent laughter as they danced. She tried to tell Marcus what was so funny, but the music was so loud. So she led him outside, where the cool air was silk on her skin, and they ended up all but making love in a taxi.

Ken St Clair picked up a dinner plate and dried it meticulously with the tea towel. Beside him, his wife pulled the plug and watched the soapy water disappear down the sink. Claudia took a towel from the hook and started to dry her hands.

She spoke tentatively, "Ken there's something we need to talk about."

Satisfied that he had done an exemplary job drying the plate, Ken placed it precisely in the sideboard before turning his attention to his wife.

"I'm pregnant," she announced.

"What?"

"I said I'm pregnant."

"Are you sure?" he asked, though he was the one who was unsure if he had heard correctly.

"Yes."

He moved to sweep his wife up into his arms. The words followed at a machine gun pace. "That's excellent. When? I mean how far gone are you?" he asked ecstatically.

"About two months I think."

"Two months! Why didn't you tell me before?"

"I wanted to be certain."

The elation swept over him and the normally staid Ken scooped his wife into his arms and showered her with kisses. Claudia accepted his kisses guardedly, fearful of the imminent difficult conversation.

"It doesn't matter. Have you seen the doctor yet? Ken asked excitedly.

"No."

"Well make an appointment. I'll take the time off and go along with you."

Claudia pulled away. "Ken we need to talk about this."

"What do you mean?"

"I want to be sure that I'm making the right decision. That **we** make the right choices."

Ken was taken aback. "Hold on now, what do you mean?"

"I'm just saying that we should think about this. Let's consider the implications and explore the options."

Ken could no longer contain his shock, "Explore the options! I can't fucking believe I'm hearing this! What options?"

"Everything Ken! What having this child now will mean? How will it affect us?"

"Claudia we've wanted a family; now we have the chance."

"I know."

"Then what? Are you seriously telling me you don't want this child?"

"No," Claudia answered wearily.

"Then what, explain it to me?"

"I don't know. I just need time."

"This is about your promotion isn't it?" Ken shouted.

"It's about *us* Ken. We have to take everything into consideration."

"Does the job mean that much to you? More than your own child?"

Claudia could not contain herself any longer. "Don't you dare Ken. In the last few weeks I've seen three young girls murdered! I've had to sit and watch the parents of a fourteen-year-old girl go to pieces when I told them that their daughter was viciously raped before being killed. I'm trying to catch the people who committed these vile acts. Yes my job does mean a lot to me."

"And you'd put your job before our child."

"Don't even go there Ken," she warned.

"I can't believe we're having this conversation. That you could even think..." He tossed down the tea towel and stormed out of the kitchen.

Claudia sat down slowly and held her head in her hands, her shoulders heaving as she began to cry silently.

Natasha gathered up her books and was making her way out of the lecture room when she felt a tap on her shoulder. She turned around to see a young, lanky, bespectacled, pony tailed male student, smiling at her.

"Hi Tasha, you're looking good. Love what you've done to your hair. I've been meaning to come to see you," he said in an effete, upper class voice.

"What for? I thought you made your position perfectly clear the last time we spoke Alex."

The man ignored Natasha's dismissal, "I don't think this is a good place to discuss things..."

"What have we got to discuss Alex?" Natasha asked sharply.

He grabbed her hand as she started to walk away, "Look maybe I was wrong, perhaps I should have given us more time."

Natasha angrily detached his hand, "No Alex, you were right. We have nothing in common. I am glad we're over. It was a mistake and I've moved on; I suggest you do too."

She walked briskly to her room in the college halls of residence, praying that Candida, her roommate, was not at home. The sight that greeted her on entering the shared flat further darkened her mood. Natasha navigated her way past discarded magazines, make-up and towels into the small kitchen. Any change of mood was dispelled by the stack of dirty dishes swimming in a sinkful of greasy water.

Fetching a half-bottle of wine from the fridge Natasha opened a cupboard to look for a clean glass, thankfully she was in luck. She felt the rush as the cold wine hit the back of her throat. It was no use; she was going to have to find a place of her own. She had changed since meeting Marcus.

It wasn't that she disliked the girl: in fact Candida could be very caring and had often lifted her spirits after a hard shift at the *Old Spotted Mare*. She was an eighteen year old away from home and having fun.

During the first term of her second year, Natasha had welcomed the outgoing up for it Candida as an ideal roommate. She had not even minded the times she had returned home to find Candida unashamedly screwing with different blokes; her bedroom door wide open. It had been Candida that had introduced her to Alex – which admittedly had seemed great then. But since meeting Marcus, things had changed so much.

Natasha heard the key turn in the front door lock as Candida bounced in, a mass of bottle blonde hair. She flung her rucksack on the empty armchair, "sorry about the mess," she gasped; already lifting the skimpy top she was wearing to reveal her huge breasts and pierced belly button. "I'll clear up when I get back tonight I promise. Guy's taking me for a drink. Are you working tonight?"

"Yes."

"Great. I mean is it okay if I bring him back here then? I think it might lead to more than just a few bevvies," Candida shouted from her bedroom.

Natasha closed her eyes and knocked back the rest of her wine. She was going to have to ask Barbara if she had any spare rooms.

"Guv, Cassie said that Jodie met this man in the *Market Tavern*. Is it just a coincidence that Andrea was also seen in there?" said Stephanie.

Claudia turned to her colleague. "What do you mean?"

"Well what if it was the same person who committed *all three* of these murders?"

"I don't see any similarities in the cases; apart from that all the victims being women."

"Not on the surface I accept, but all three women were brutally beaten, and all three visited the *Market Tavern*. What if they had met someone in the pub and left with them? That would answer why there was no sign of a break-in at Andrea's wouldn't it."

Claudia let the notion sink into her brain. "Let's go back to the station and look over the Napier Court files."

Marcus and the rest of his trainee colleagues were in a city pub having a celebratory drink. *Fast Love* by George Michael played in the background, competing with the numerous loud conversations.

Olivia tapped Marcus on the shoulder. "Everybody's going back to Tracy's. Are you coming?"

"I'm not sure."

"Come on you can't be a party pooper," Olivia baited. "Is your girlfriend down this week?"

"No."

"Well what's the problem? You don't want to be sat alone watching TV on a Friday night do you?"

"I suppose not."

"Besides, she's probably in the student bar herself as we speak. Or can't you trust yourself?" Olivia dared.

Marcus sipped his drink as Olivia took his arm and met no resistance.

"Good. You're coming. Don't worry, I'll look after you."

Stephanie ran her fingers across the statement, her eyes widening as she read. She spun on the chair to face Claudia. "Guv, listen to this." She read a passage from the statement to Claudia.

"That puts him in the *Market Tavern* on the same day as Jodie," Claudia said as she stood up. "Get your coat Steph."

Chapter 16

Natasha closed the book shut and swung her legs from the single bed. She eased her feet into the trainers, tied up the laces, then left her room and headed towards the JCR. She crossed the quadrangle, ignoring the few boisterous students larking on the lawn, approached the notice board and searched down the names listed alphabetically. Natasha smiled contentedly when hers finally appeared under the heading of reserves. Okay so she hadn't made the first squad, that would have been too much to expect, but at least she was in.

Turning around, Natasha zipped up her tracksuit top and set off on a slow jog. She headed outside the college campus and opened her stride as she followed her now familiar route. On the wave of euphoria, Natasha managed to complete her daily run in a new record time. As she walked back through the college gates, she saw Alex chatting with a group of first year girls. She pulled her shoulders back and continued purposefully on her way; even he couldn't spoil her mood.

The posse of reporters and cameramen that had gathered outside the house on the thriving council estate were concentrating on the drawn curtains when the door opened. Claudia and Stephanie emerged flanking a young man; his head covered by a blanket, as they fought their way to a parked police car.

The crowd that had gathered began shouting, "Kill the fucking nonce!", "Child molester!" and "Beast!" as they bayed for blood.

Claudia ushered Stephanie into the car, turned and strode to face the rush of reporters as microphones and recorders were thrust in her face.

"Are you charging him Inspector?" A TV reporter shouted.

"There will be a full press release this afternoon," Claudia bellowed over the yelling as things started to turn into a melee.

Even though he had spent over an hour getting ready, carefully applying cocoa butter, baby lotion, Vaseline, hair oil and finally aftershave, Marcus tugged at the sleeve of his suit nervously in a display of first day nerves.

The portly man who had interviewed Marcus before the start of the course opened his office door and strode over to Marcus. Even the short walk from his office had left the man out of breath. His chubby fingers formed into a handshake, which he extended to Marcus.

"I'll introduce you to the rest of the staff first and then we'll sort you out with a car," he wheezed.

After a brief rest to recover from his efforts, he finally heaved his hulking body from the desk and with great lumbering strides, led Marcus through to the modern office in the main building. Marcus smiled politely as he was presented to the predominantly female staff who acted as clerical support for the team of installers.

Claudia waited until Stephanie had inserted the tapes into the machine. On the other side of the table, a nervous young man sat beside his Asian lawyer whose suit had seen better days.

"Are you ready?" she asked as Stephanie took her seat.

The young man nodded silently. Stephanie pressed the play button and waited whilst Claudia spoke into the machine.

"Interview of Darren Turner. Present are Detective Inspector Claudia St Clair."

"Detective Constable Stephanie Elford."

Claudia pointed to Darren, who gave his name, then pointed towards the solicitor.

"Uthmaan Iqbal."

Introductions complete, Claudia relaxed in her seat and began the interview.

"Darren can you tell me what happened on the night of ...."

"I didn't mean to kill her," Darren began softly.

Claudia shot the solicitor a look.

"I advised my client that he doesn't have to answer any questions. My client wants to cooperate. He insists."

"Do you understand why I have to make sure you are clear of what you are doing Darren?"

"I know. I'm not a monster." He looked directly into Claudia's eyes. "It started when one of the lads from the estate saw me in the shop and started laughing. He told his mates that I was a child molester. I thought he was just trying to get me to bite, so I ignored it. Then I heard a few more of them saying it, calling me a kiddie fiddler when they saw me. I had enough and fronted them. That was when they told me that someone had seen me going round with a fourteen-year-old girl. When I told them that it was all lies, one of them told me that his cousin was in the same class as her."

"I thought it couldn't be true. I mean I met her at a pub in Blackheath. She told me she was eighteen." He looked apologetically into Claudia's eyes. "I didn't know she was only fourteen. Honest."

"Anyway, I arranged to meet her *that* night. I just wanted her to tell me it was all lies. She just laughed; just laughed - do you know how that felt? She said that I hadn't cared when I was sleeping with her, so why should it matter now?"

The tears started to form. He waited a moment to compose himself then continued. "I told her that I couldn't go out with her anymore. She said it was no big deal."

"Then she turned nuts, saying things she shouldn't have said."

"What did she say Darren?" Claudia coaxed.

"That she had had better sex on her own anyway, that I was crap in bed. Evil, vicious things. If she hadn't said what she did, I wouldn't have got mad."

"She turned all nasty. Told me that I was a pussy, that perhaps I was gay," he looked up, "I 'm not gay."

He began to cry. "I only wanted to show her I was not gay. But it got out of hand. She started kissing me, touching me, then when we were doing it she started laughing at me again, asked me if it was in yet.

"I just lost it and hit her, but she wouldn't stop laughing," Darren muttered through the tears, wiping his streaming nose on his jacket. "I didn't mean to hurt her," he cried.

Claudia walked through the living room door and took a seat beside her husband. After listening to Darren's harrowing confession, she needed someone to unload on.

"Hold me please Ken," Claudia said. "It's not that I don't want this baby. You know that; please believe me."

"Then what is it Claudia?"

"I'm afraid Ken," she said and burst into tears.

"That's okay darling, it's understandable. It's the hormones," he consoled taking her into his arms.

"Ken, if you'd seen half the things I have, you would know what I mean Ken. Who has the right to bring a child into this world?"

Marcus lay on the bed jingling the keys into the phone.

"Yes, it's only a Vectra," he said smugly.

"Listen to yourself. It's a car Marcus!"

"I know. The mileage allowance is a bit low."

"You can't have everything. Just be grateful you've got a job and a car!"

"Guess where I'm going to be next week?"

"Where?"

"Nottingham."

"Honest?"

"Yes. So I can see you all week. That is if you want to."

"Oh Marcus of course I do. That's excellent."

"Yes, and they pay for me to stay in a hotel."

Claudia steeled herself then knocked on the door and walked into Superintendent Middleton's office.

"Can I have a word sir?"

"Of course Claudia. Have a seat."

"Thank you."

"What is it?"

"I need to take some leave."

"What's the matter? Not the Mason case? You did a good job

"No sir, I'm going to have a baby."

Chapter 17

Marcus opened the glove compartment of the Vectra, rumbled amongst the tapes until he was satisfied with his choice. He inserted it into the player and sat back while the tape fast-forwarded until Roberta Flack & Donny Hathaway started singing *Back Together*. A grin spread across his face. His fingers tapped out the beat on the steering wheel as he sang along with the tape, every now and then managing to hit the right note in the right key.

The song was starting to fade out when Marcus saw the familiar shape alighting from the bus. He opened the passenger door as Natasha spotted the car and began walking towards him. She got in, tossed a bag onto the back seat and kissed him.

Marcus put the car into gear and smoothly pulled away. They drove for ten minutes, thankful for the light traffic and, aided by Natasha's competent navigating, Marcus found the Travelodge hotel situated five miles from the city centre without incident. He brought the Vectra to a stop in one of the allocated parking spaces beside the small green hedgerows in front of the brown three-storey building.

Marcus and Natasha walked through the lobby of the hotel to the reception. The male receptionist smiled and winked knowingly as he confirmed that a *single room* had indeed been booked for Marcus, who signed and collected the keys.

He slid the cardkey down the computerised gizmo and flung open the door. Natasha dropped her bag, threw herself to Marcus, and gave him a hungry kiss.

Claudia opened the drawer of her desk and started clearing out the contents, her head full of differing thoughts – most of which involved uncertainty. She thought of the many female colleagues she had witnessed in the position she now faced. The vast majority had returned from their maternity leave changed people. Children did that; they had a tendency to make mothers revise their priorities. That thought alone was enough to make her shudder. Whichever way she looked at it, her career was going to change. It was a frightening thought.

You had to be unselfish to raise children, make the kind of sacrifices and compromises *her* mother had.

A knock on the door interrupted her thoughts.

"Come in," Claudia said, looking up to see Taff and Stephanie.

"Taff, Stephanie," she smiled.

Taff spoke first, "we wanted to say all the best - you know away from the others."

"Thank you Taff."

"It was great working with you."

"That goes for me too," said Stephanie.

"Yes. Shame we never closed the Napier Court case," Claudia smiled.

"To be honest guv, you can't be surprised. I don't reckon this was deliberate. My gut feelings say the only way that they'll solve this one is by chance or unless whoever did it is daft enough to kill again. Sometimes we lose. Fact of life - can't be helped," Taff said.

"I'd like to say thanks for recommending me for promotion."

"Anything to help. You did a good job on the Mason case."

"Well anyway I appreciate it. Thanks and good luck," said Stephanie unable to resist adding "By the way chanting is *really* soothing for unborn babies."

"And you. Don't forget - girl power!"

The two women laughed in unison as the Welshman shook his head.

Marcus entered the three-storey head office of Hamilton, Knights & Robey and approached the young mixed-race receptionist.

"Hello, I'm here to see Ms Ferris."

"If you take a seat I'll buzz her. Who shall I tell her is waiting?"

"Mr Carpenter. Marcus Carpenter."

The receptionist said "thank you," politely; picked up her phone and spoke briefly to someone on the other end then replaced the handset. "Mrs Ferris is on her way down," she informed Marcus.

"Thanks."

A few moments later, a pretty, petite blonde in a suit came out of the lift. She walked straight over to Marcus.

"Mr Carpenter, I'm Tanya Ferris. Come on, I'll take you up to the office," she smiled.

They entered the lift, the doors closing slowly as Tanya pushed the button for the third floor and leant back. The door closed noiselessly and there was a whirring noise as the lift rose.

"How long do you think it will take you to install the new kit?" Tanya asked trying to break the tense silence.

"I hope I'll be finished by Friday; but it could be next week," Marcus replied.

A light flashed to indicate their arrival at each floor before a bell sounded and the lift door opened smoothly. Tanya allowed Marcus out and led him down a carpeted hall, passing offices that housed various clerical staff, until they arrived at a room that contained a desk and a comfortable black leather swivel chair.

"You can use this office while you're here. Put your stuff down and I'll show you where everything is," Tanya said.

"Thanks."

Marcus was in his temporary office busily working at the computer screen, when there was a knock on the door and Tanya entered.

"How's it going?" she asked, closing the door behind her.

"So far so good," Marcus replied.

Tanya moved to sit on the corner of the desk, the short skirt revealing more than a glimpse of leg, which caught Marcus unaware. His eyes remained on her legs causing him to blush guiltily.

Tanya smiled noting Marcus' reaction. "Is there anything you need?"

"No, I think I'm managing okay," he said, regaining his composure.

"It must be a bit lonely working here alone. Some of us go to the pub for lunch every now and then. It's not that expensive and it's handy. We were wondering if you wanted to join us today?"

After eating in a hotel alone for the past few days, the thought of a warm meal in the company of others seemed a welcome change for Marcus. "I'd love to," he answered.

"Great, come on then."

164

The pub was nothing like the *Market Tavern* thought Marcus as he carried his 'freshly cooked cod and chips' to the table and sat beside Tanya. The two men and the woman that sat around the table were laughing.

"So, where are you from?" the oldest of the group asked.

"I live in Blackheath, London."

"What's life like in London?"

"Much the same as anywhere I else I guess," Marcus answered, picking up his knife and cutting the fish into a biteable size.

The hour passed by largely with Marcus being ribbed by the three workers who all considered Londoners boastful, brash and self-centred. 'Not at all friendly like people from round here' had been the expression. Short from calling him a 'Southern softie', they had managed to explore all the usual stereotypes.

The others ate quickly whilst Marcus answered their questions. He had not finished his meal when they decided they were heading back.

"Off you go, I'll wait with Marcus and show him the way back," Tanya said.

Five minutes later, fish meal completed, Marcus and Tanya left the pub and walked back to the office.

"Sorry about that," she apologised, "not everyone thinks like them. I mean, I wouldn't be averse to spending a weekend in London every now and then."

Marcus let the comment ride, responding, "it's not all its cracked up to be. Nobody has time for anyone else."

They reached Marcus' office and Tanya followed him inside, watching as he removed his jacket and hung it behind the leather chair.

"Do you have to drive back to London every night?" she asked.

"It depends. For some jobs they put me up in a hotel."

"Oh right. Are you in a hotel while you're down here?"

"Yes."

"Must be a bit of a bind living out of a suitcase; Christ, conferences are bad enough."

"I'm quite new to it so it doesn't bother me."

"I'd go crazy."

"Not me."

Tanya smiled, "Oh well, better get some work done. See you. Don't forget to shout if you need anything." She hopped off the desk, making a scene out of smoothing her dress and left Marcus to return to his work.

Taff Morgan picked up the two drinks and carefully made his way to the table his daughter had snagged. As he placed her glass in front of her, she lifted a tiny article out of the bag.

"Do you like my skirt?" she asked him.

"There's not enough material there for a belt. You can't possibly be serious Laura."

"Dad this is a skirt, look," Laura said, standing and holding the narrow mini skirt to her waist.

"Sit down Laura, you're embarrassing me," Taff said looking around the pub to see who was taking interest in her impromptu fashion show. He caught sight of a familiar face and quickly turned back to his daughter.

"God dad, you're worse than mum."

As she took a sip of her drink, Laura noticed that the black woman beside the bar was watching their table. She seemed to be eyeing up her dad. A wicked thought came into her head. She waited, keeping her eye on the woman, who in turn was definitely keeping an eye on her dad. She engaged her father in insignificant small talk, surreptitiously watching the bar. When the woman left to go to the Ladies, Laura knocked back the rest of her drink.

"Can I have another please dad?"

She waited until he stood up. The woman opened the door for the Ladies. Laura got up, "I'll be back in a minute," she said and hurried off.

On the other side of the door, Laura found herself in an Edwardian barn of a loo with five cubicles and a row of porcelain sinks that looked about a hundred years' old.

Three basins along, the black woman who had been eyeing up her father stood in front of the mirror fixing her hair. The woman was pretty, probably in her thirties – not that she was good at guessing ages. Improvising wildly, Laura confidently strode to the sink next to her, rummaged in her bag, and waved an emery board in the air as evidence.

Taking a deep gulp, Laura launched into a breathless chatter. "Oh my God! I can't believe it! I thought I'd broken a nail! And I haven't!"

"Lucky you," Melishia replied casually, knowing full well that this was just a clumsy attempt to engage her in conversation. Was Taff's daughter (Christ you would have to be a moron not to have detected the resemblance) going to ask for the loan of a pound coin, the use of her mobile, or what other favour? Her opening gambit had not been subtle.

Laura blushed while she examined her index finger, as if she and the hand had just been introduced.

Taff reclaimed his seat, took a sip of his pint while he waited for his daughter. He felt sure Laura was up to something. Always the minx, yet equally he had always felt he could rely on the girl. When she focused, really set her mind to something, her achievements could be remarkable. She went clubbing, incessantly it seemed, but she never let up on that athletics training. Had the medals to prove it. She wasn't ambitious in the same way as her sister, just coasted along at school, doing well enough and not too much more.

Yet she had the commonsense. Sometimes he had found himself talking about the job with her, even when she was a ten-year-old. She grasped the practicalities; had a natural flair for handling genuine emergencies with calm; she was direct, she had courage. For all the false nails and daft skirts - there was a sense of responsibility that he was proud of.

Laura stuffed the emery board away. Whatever the problem was, thought Melishia, it had nothing to do with manicures.

"Excuse me, have you any lipstick I could borrow?" the girl asked, making an exaggerated display of ruffling her hair.

Melishia suppressed a laugh as she handed across her tube of lipstick.

"I don't mean to be rude. But to be honest, I couldn't help seeing you looking at my dad. I know my dad better than he realizes. I could tell he fancied you. I really could. I think he wanted to speak to you but he won't, because I'm in the way. Or maybe he thought you were waiting to meet someone," said Laura.

"Its just that he is such a nice man, and for some strange reason I think you two could be good together. Will you please come back and have a drink with us?"

Melishia, who had been in so many weird situations, felt her jaw drop. It was hypnotizing. She closed her mouth, and went on listening to the girl. It wouldn't have been easy to get a word in edgeways.

Laura was watching the woman's face all the time she talked, meeting her eyes, and with an instinctive talent for reading people, she thought *"so far, so good."*

"You see, I need to leave in a couple of minutes. I've just had a text from my friend and it's very, very important for me to meet her. Way over at Earls Court. So you'd be doing me a big favour. Are you coming?" Laura said, pushing the door and holding it open, to let Melishia follow behind her.

Taff watched his younger daughter bounce through the heavy swing door with its international 'Ladies' symbol – head, arms, legs, and triangular skirt, like a paper doll. His heart skipped a beat when she turned her head and said something unintelligible to the woman behind her. He watched unmoved as the pair made their way to his table.

"Dad, this is Melishia; my friend from college's mum. Do you mind if she joins us?" Laura said innocently.

Taff stood and held out his hand, "Hello Melishia,"

"Sorry, I didn't mean to intrude, but your daughter is very persuasive," Melishia said accepting the handshake, her eyes pleading a request for forgiveness.

"Don't be daft; you're not intruding is she dad?"

"Not at all, please join us," said Taff awkwardly, watching Laura almost dragging the poor Melishia into the seat between her and her father.

Laura smiled triumphantly. "Where's your manners dad? Melishia hasn't got a drink. Tell you what, you give me the money and I'll go to the bar," she said already rising.

"I'm sorry," Melishia apologised once Laura had left for the bar. "I didn't know what to say to her. I haven't told her that I know you."

"I knew she was up to something," Taff smiled. Melishia looked stunning. Her rust-red shirt made her dark skin glow and the skirt she wore skimmed instead of clinging lasciviously to her body. "I haven't seen you around for a while, must be years now. How are you?"

"Good."

"It shows."

"I'm not the same person you knew then Taff. My life has changed."

Laura returned and handed the glass of white wine to Melishia and winked to her dad as she pocketed the change.

Melishia watched incredulously as Laura made a display of answering the phone, standing up and moving slightly away, nodding her head as she uttered a few "Calm downs," before turning off the mobile phone. "Bugger, I've got to go dad. Carly's been dumped by her boyfriend. She's in a right state," she announced, bending down and gathering her bags.

Taff stood to accompany his daughter.

"Dad I said I'll meet her by the station. There's no need for you to come along. I'll phone you later. See you again Melishia," and was off before any protest could be made.

Friday afternoon found Marcus working in front of a computer screen when Tanya opened the door.

"How much longer do you think you'll be?" she asked.

Marcus looked at his watch; it was five-thirty already. "I can finish off now if you're ready to leave."

"The building is almost empty."

"It doesn't matter; I'm going to have to come back on Monday anyway." Marcus said, shutting down his computer and starting to pack up.

"Actually I was wondering if you'd fancy a drink. I've got a little time before my bus is due."

Marcus hesitated. "I'm not sure."

"Okay. I just thought I'd ask." Tanya flashed him a warm smile.

"Wait a minute. Why not?" Marcus said, grabbing his jacket.

Even before she inserted the key in the lock, Natasha could hear the loud music. The last thing she needed after a heavy shift at work was a late night. With a feeling of trepidation, she opened the door and made her way inside, where Candida lay on the sofa, her lap in Guy's head and a glass of vodka in her hand.

Candida raised her head from its resting place, looked up at Natasha through glazed eyes and smiled, "Alex get 'Tasha a glass, she looks totally knackered."

Natasha spun her head and saw Alex grinning drunkenly behind the door.

"It's okay. I'm bushed. I think I'll crash now thanks."

"Oh come on Natasha where's your manners? One glass just to be sociable."

Although, Natasha felt like telling the pompous idiot to get lost, there was no way she was going to give him the satisfaction of letting him get her rattled. She accepted the glass politely as she took off her coat and sank into the armchair.

"So how's your love life Natasha?" Alex asked, taking a perch beside her on the armrest.

"None of your business Alex," she said dismissively.

"Touchy. Is that frustration I detect?"

"Shut up Alex. Tasha has a boyfriend back in London," warned Candida.

"You can't blame a man for trying," Alex smiled.

"Just chill man," Guy said as he leaned forward and offered Natasha a spliff. "Here Natasha, try this it's high grade. Seriously good."

Even though 'chilling' was the furthest thing on her mind, Natasha took a gulp from the glass, reached out her hand and accepted the spliff.

Claudia stood up, smoothed down her skirt and followed the usher through the doors into the court. As she entered the witness box, she could feel all the eyes directed at her. She spotted Katherine Mason her face drawn and tired. Far away from her she noticed Mrs Turner alongside her husband.

Claudia thought how tragic and painful it was for both mothers in such different ways. For Katherine Mason, there would be the ongoing knowledge that she would never see her daughter again, that her life had been taken away so early. She would be denied the experience of watching her daughter growing into a woman, perhaps walking down the aisle or becoming a mother. Because of this tragedy, Katherine Mason might never be a grandmother.

Darren's mother in turn would have to live with the guilt that the son she had given birth to and raised with all her love had killed another human being.

The day that she had knocked on the Turner's door and had informed the shocked woman that her son was going to be charged with the murder of Jodie Mason, had been one of the worse tasks Claudia had ever carried out.

Claudia picked up the Bible and followed the words being spoken by the usher, "I solemnly swear to tell the truth, the whole truth ...."

Natasha woke up with the mother of all hangovers: the night before nothing but a blur. She remembered getting in, the drinking and smoking; then nothing afterwards.

She flung the duvet from the bed, raised herself up jadedly and took in the image that reflected in the mirror. God she looked like shit! Glancing down beside her bed, she saw her knickers. Almost in slow motion, Natasha dropped her hand, picked them up and with great effort managed to drag herself from the bed. Her legs felt heavy as she walked across the room, dropped her knickers into her laundry basket before taking her bathrobe from its hook and wrapping it around her weary body.

After twenty minutes in a soothing hot bath, her mood had brightened and as she towelled her hair dry, she reached for the phone.

Marcus held the phone to his ear awkwardly as he dried himself with the large bath sheet, a souvenir from the hotel in Nottingham.

"I'm going to see the solicitor tomorrow," he said into the earpiece.

"Good luck."

"Thanks. About next week, when shall I pick you up?"

"I'm not sure yet. I'll phone you as soon as I know," said Natasha

"Okay."

"Look I've got to go now. I've managed to get some extra shifts this week. I'll phone you tomorrow. Love you," she said, hurriedly ending the conversation.

"Love you too." Marcus said and heard the click as Natasha hung up.

Darren heard the brutally loud alarm bell followed by the sounds of men frantically rushing around. He watched as the Prison Officers sprinted to an open cell. Darren hurriedly followed the action, trying to peer inside to get a clear view, but was roughly shoved aside as the urgency rose amongst the officers and the cell door was hastily slammed.

After a matter of minutes, the seriousness of the situation became apparent as prisoners on association were hastily herded back into their respective cells.

Behind his cell door, Darren closed his eyes as he recalled the sight of the young prisoner being brought down from the window, his face a horrible shade of blue. He'd had a glimpse of hell. The tears began to run down his cheeks as he envisioned the next few miserable years of his life. However deep and bitter his remorse, he knew he did not deserve this - not for having big workman's hands and more strength in them than he realized.

Marcus parked the Vectra outside the semi-detached house. He remained in the car for a while, summoning up the courage. He finally got out of the car, walked up to the house, rang the doorbell and waited apprehensively.

A striking black woman dressed in tight jeans and T-shirt opened the door. Behind his mother, a small boy looked on.

"Daddy," the boy squealed excitedly, running to the door when he recognised Marcus.

Maxine's arm shot out to hold back her son. "Monju get back inside," she ordered firmly.

The boy halted and disappointedly retreated back inside, giving Marcus a smile and wave hidden from his mother.

"What do you want?" snapped a hostile Maxine.

"Can I come inside?"

"No. Say what you've got to say from there," she spat.

"I want to sort everything out," Marcus said.

"There's nothing to sort out."

"I only want to see my son Maxine."

"It's not going to happen. You've had your chance."

"Look, I'm not here to fight Maxine. I'm working now, I've got my life back together. Can't we be adult about this?"

Maxine crossed her arms defiantly, "Don't come to my house and tell me.."

"Your house?"

"Yes. *My* fucking house. Don't bother coming round again."

"I didn't come to argue Maxine. I was hoping that you would be reasonable. If you can't see sense, then I'll go to a solicitor," Marcus said.

"Good, do that. I'll go and see one too! Now you're working you can start paying me more maintenance! Don't try and mess with me Marcus; you'll lose!"

She slammed the door shut. Marcus walked back to his car. As he switched on the ignition Monju's face appeared at the window; he waved lovingly to his father, but the gesture was cut short when Maxine drew the curtain.

Taff picked up the phone and hesitantly dialled the number written on the scrap of paper, wondering if this was a foolish thing to do. The writing was neat, with swirls and loops that an expert would no doubt suggest revealed openness. Finally, a voice answered.

"Are you busy?" he asked. No small talk. He wrote down the instructions and picked up his car keys.

Twenty minutes later, Taff locked his car, grabbed the bottle of brandy he had bought on impulse and walked towards the house at the end of the terrace. He rang the bell and saw a light come on inside.

Taff took in Melishia's home. It was surprisingly 'down-to-earth', nothing like what he would have pictured for the woman he had got to know so long ago. Books were neatly stacked in a pine flat pack bookcase. He bent down and studied some, again surprised at the number of psychology, sociology and counselling titles that nestled alongside Maya Angelou, Alice Walker, Toni Morrison and others.

Melishia walked out of the kitchen, set the two glasses on top of the smoked glass table, poured two generous portions of brandy and handed one across to the Welshman.

"Cheers," he said raising his glass. "Nice place; must cost a bomb to rent."

Melishia smiled, took a swig of her drink, "I told you my life has changed. How long has it been? Five or six years?"

"More like ten, I think."

"As long as that?" she said shaking her head as she reflected, "I lost a lot of time, I'm clean now. And I own this."

"I've got to say you look better for the change. What happened?"

Melishia fluttered her hands above her head, like a Gospel preacher. "I *saw* the light!" she told him, a little light-heartedly.

"Like hell."

Her voice changed to a sombre tone. "It *was* like hell when my friend Louise died the way she did a few years ago. I don't think you knew her, she was my best friend, absolute stunner. She had my back and I had hers. Anyway, one night, at the Players Club, she let this punter take her off partying without telling me who he was, where they were going, when she'd be in touch. He was just *so* rich-looking she couldn't resist; broke all the rules. Louise hadn't been having much luck at the time. Her habit was getting bigger, which led to other health problems. Louise had lost her sense of risk, I think. She was getting desperate."

"So when this guy in his flash designer suit appeared and started paying her attention, it was obvious she was going to accept the invitation. I saw it brewing from the corner of my eye. Louise called me over, said he wanted another girl. He took one look at me and made me feel like shit, whispered in my ear that he was looking for a

174

white girl, not a black whore. Whatever he had in mind I was glad I was going to be no part of it."

"I shouldn't have let her go. I told her there was danger in the man's eyes, but she wouldn't have any of it."

"I went to the toilets, and when I came back they'd gone. That was a Saturday night. She phoned me the next Monday." Melishia shook her head as she relived the painful memory. "I will never forget that call. She could barely speak; sounded like a wounded puppy. It took her twenty minutes to find out where she was. I got in a cab and went to her."

Melishia reached for the bottle, topped up her glass and caught her breath.

"They had brought her to an empty storage lot at the back of an industrial estate in Park Royal. She was barely alive. They had beaten her and left her there to die. There was so much blood. I called the ambulance and held her in my arms telling her she would be fine. By the time the ambulance arrived, she was dead."

Taff listened, stunned in spite of his long and intimate acquaintance with the dark side.

"She can't have been murdered," he said respectfully. "I'd know."

Melishia shook her head. "No, there was an inquest. The verdict was Death by Misadventure. They said that the beating could have been a contributory factor, but it was the overdose that killed her. A cocktail of drugs. Strangely enough they said if she hadn't been out of it, she would have apparently felt more pain."

"And what did you do then?"

Melishia leaned back against the sofa and shut her eyes pensively.

"I had a bit of a breakdown myself. Stopped working, sat at home and cried. Then I went to the GPC clinic at the hospital, because I hadn't had a normal GP since I was about fourteen. I told them I wanted to clean up. I cried; I talked about Louise. I'd gone without gear for two days so I was hysterical. You know what; I was in rehab a week later."

"And then?"

"It wasn't that simple, I didn't get clean overnight. I stayed in rehab for well over a year, became close to the staff and started helping them out with the other patients.

"When I was strong enough to leave, I decided that I wanted to help other 'working girls' who wanted to get out of the life. I did a couple of days a week as a volunteer in the rehab and in return, they got me on some relevant courses – you know counselling, advice and stuff. The rest of the week, I would go out on the streets and offer the girls any help I could."

"Well one thing led to another. You know what they say say? 'Education, education, education'. So I went and got me some. Then I managed to sweet-talk the Council into funding a project to help get girls off the street, would you believe that. Now I'm qualified and managing the Project which is doing great."

"I'm awed," said Taff simply. Inside he was thrilled. Maybe in some small way his request for a lesson in texting had played some part in Melishia's new career.

"Can I talk about me for a minute?" he said.

"Course you can, honey. Let me get us another drink."

"I'm working on a murder case, and I was hoping you could help me."

"Me. How?"

"One of the victims was on the game. Not working the streets, but I thought you might know of her. A mixed-race woman called Andrea Bailey. She was found dead in her apartment in Napier Court, Blackheath."

Melishia shook her head. "*That* case; it was in the news for a while wasn't it? Can't say I recognise or know anything about her. I could ask around for you."

"I'd appreciate it," said Taff.

She passed across the refilled glass. "I've often wondered what happened to you." She let the brandy warm in her hands. "You never looked down on us, hassled us or tried it on with any of us."

"Not my style."

"I wish you had. Did you know I had a thing for you?"

Marcus slid into the booth beside Tanya. The busy city pub was packed with office workers, a large group of whom were obviously celebrating a birthday, which meant that the pair was not given much attention.

"I bet you have a few adventures on you travels?" Tanya said in between sips of her Jack Daniels and coke.

176

"Not really, I've only been doing this job for a few weeks and I'm involved with somebody."

Tanya smiled temptingly "That's the beauty of your job isn't it? No one's ever going to know who you've met on your travels."

Marcus shrugged "I never really thought about that before," he said, finishing his drink and signalling to her, "Would you like another?"

"I really shouldn't, but what the hell!"

Marcus made his way to the bar and returned with fresh drinks. He handed Tanya her glass.

"Thank you."

"So what about you? Are you in a relationship?" Marcus asked.

Tanya held up her ring finger. "Three years down the road. Does it bother you?"

"Should it?"

"Not in my mind. As they say; what he doesn't know won't hurt him."

Marcus smiled.

"What are you doing tonight then?" Tanya asked, making her offer plain.

"I've got to go back to London."

"Pity. Can't you get out of going back till tomorrow?"

Marcus shook his head "I don't think so. Give me your mobile number and if I can sort it, I'll give you a ring. I'm back on Monday anyway."

Tanya smiled as she wrote her number on a piece of a paper and passed it across to Marcus.

Marcus closed the door and started to undress. As he emptied his pockets, he found the piece of paper with Tanya's number on it. He shook his head and flopped onto the bed. He screwed the piece of paper into a ball, tossed it into the bin then reached across the small bedside table, picked up the handset and dialled Natasha's number.

"Hello," a male voice answered.

"Is Natasha there?"

"No I'm afraid she isn't. Can I take a message?"

"Can you just tell her that Marcus phoned."

"Of course. I've heard much about you. I thought you were a figment of her imagination. My name is Alex."

"I'm sorry, I don't know what you mean."

"Natasha and I were an item last term. We're still close and I wondered how you felt about her."

"That's none of your business."

Alex detected the concern in Marcus' voice. A grin spread across his face. "Relax man, I'm just trying to be nice. Look from what I've heard you're quite a lot older than her."

"What's that to do with you?" Marcus asked testily.

"Well that depends. If this thing between you is just a fling, I'd like to know. It doesn't sound like anything with a future does it?"

"Listen mate, what happens between Natasha and me is our business."

Alex knew he had the man worried. Like a dog with a bone, he refused to let the issue go. "That's not exactly true. You see, I think Natasha and I might be getting back together."

After a minute of silence, Alex spoke again. "Are you still there? I didn't mean to upset you. I'll make sure she gets your message."

Marcus slammed the receiver down angrily before he said anything he might regret. What the fuck did that bloke mean and why hadn't Natasha mentioned him? The bile started to rise in his stomach at the possibility that once again he had been betrayed.

Darren watched over the landing rails as the officers opened up the remaining cells on the wing for association. It was the first time Darren had ventured outside the small single cell he had been transferred to since being placed under the notorious 'Rule 43' after being identified as a 'vulnerable prisoner'.

It wasn't a move that he had welcomed, but after being attacked when the nature of his offence had spread round the prison; the choice had been taken out of his hands.

Darren spotted the badly dyed hair of the man that had tried to hang himself. He walked quickly down the iron stairs, caught up with the man and tapped him on the shoulder.

"Are you okay?" he asked, determined to get acquainted with his fellow sufferer. They seemed to be roughly the same age and from what Darren had overheard, were facing similar futures. A lengthy period of derision, fear and danger lay ahead for both.

"What's it to you?" he said defensively, staring absently at Darren through lifeless green eyes. Darren guessed he had been placed on medication that kept him placid.

"I saw them taking you to the hospital wing. Someone said that you tried to kill yourself."

"Well, didn't work again did it."

Darren pulled his tobacco pouch from his pocket and held it out, "My name's Darren, want a smoke?"

Over the next few days, Darren spent as much time with the only person on the wing who understood what he was going through. Darren learned that Jack had tried to hang himself twice before. They discussed the future - or rather the lack of it and exchanged views on the best way to put themselves out of their misery.

"The next time I'm going to slash my wrists," Jack said.

Natasha waited in the lodge as Harry the porter made his way to the window. He handed across three envelopes to Natasha and returned to reading the racing pages of his newspaper.

She walked back to her room and was reading her mail when she heard the front door slam. As usual, Candida's entrance was dramatic.

"Tasha are you in?" she yelled, barging into Natasha's bedroom.

Natasha looked up. When she saw the expression on Candida's face, she placed the letter back inside the envelope.

"What's the matter?" she asked.

"Give me two minutes," Candida said and left the bewildered Natasha alone. When she returned, she was holding two glasses full of wine. She passed one to Natasha and sat on the edge of the bed. It was now that Natasha began to feel uneasy.

Candida took a swig of the wine, "look there's no easy way to say this."

"What is it Candida?"

"It's Alex. The shit's been spreading rumours. He's telling everybody that he shagged you last week."

"He's been saying what?"

"I know. I saw him talking to three first year students. When I got near, he spotted me and was off. He looked as guilty as hell so I thought he was talking about me; the snobby dickhead," she paused to take another sip of wine.

"Anyway I asked the girls what they had been talking about and Emily Forrester – you know she hates me – took great pride in telling me that Alex had told them that he had been shagging you. I wanted to slap the smug grin off her face."

Thoughts ran through Natasha's head. The vodka, the skunk; waking up in the morning and finding her knickers on the floor. Had she really slept with him that night when she was wrecked and oblivious of the fact? She took a large gulp from the glass.

"What happened last Tuesday Candida?"

"Don't be silly Tasha. Nothing happened between you. I am positive of that. The little shit's just stirring."

Candida's words did not reassure Natasha.

"Honest Tasha nothing happened. The reason I was suspicious was that I thought he was telling them what *really* happened that night."

That brought Natasha from her thoughts.

"What do you mean. What happened?"

"Well after you left, Guy and me started fooling around, then Guy suggested Alex join in...."

Natasha's mouth dropped open.

"Don't say anything, I know it was a dumb thing to do. It was the skunk. I mean I hadn't had a threesome before and it seemed fun. Not that it was all that great to be honest."

If her thoughts hadn't been elsewhere, Natasha would have laughed at her flatmates flippant candidness.

Candida put the wine glass down on the floor, placed her arm around Natasha's shoulder, and gave her a hug.

Candida took a deep breath. "Listen Tasha that's not the problem. After I told Alex what I thought about him, he went berserk. He said he had spoken to Marcus. He was yelling that it was only a matter of time before he got back with you."

"What!"

"I don't know what he said to Marcus, but I'm sure it wasn't good."

Chapter 18

Marcus squeezed some baby lotion into his palm, then rubbed it on his body, his mind pre-occupied, wondering whether to call Natasha.

That brief telephone conversation with the snotty bloke had been gnawing away at him ever since. Why hadn't she said anything about him?

He opened a can of beer and tuned into a late night chat show on TV. He listened as people talked about how an affair had affected their life. He remembered Natasha's words, "I won't be unfaithful. I promise you." Empty words.

Marcus watched until the advertisement break, then picked up his mobile phone and dialled a number.

"Hello."

"It's Marcus. Can you talk?"

"Not really," Tanya replied.

"Is your husband there?"

"Yes."

Marcus removed one of the jiffy envelopes from under the pillow and opened it; spreading the notes over the bed. Each envelope had contained ten thousand pounds. Fifty thousand pounds; less the money he had paid out for the impending revamp of the flat.

Now that he was working, it was going to be easy to deposit the cash into his bank account slowly without attracting attention. He smiled. He had already opened an account in Monju's name with some of the money from one envelope.

"I've been thinking about you," he said, his eyes firmly on the TV

Tanya curled her legs in the chair, "Have you?" she purred.

"Does the offer still stand?"

Tanya looked across at her husband who was concentrating on his TV programme, "Yes".

Marcus touched the blanket of notes, "Okay, I'll speak to you on Monday."

"That's fine, see you on Monday."

"Bye."

"Bye."

Marcus tossed down his mobile, walked to the TV and angrily switched it off. "Fucking no good whore!" he yelled.

Ken St Clair drove his Mercedes into the car park of the small private hospital. He opened his door, walked round to help a clearly pregnant Claudia out of the passenger door, and led her to the reception.

"Mr and Mrs St Clair. We've an appointment for a scan," Ken said proudly.

Tanya entered Marcus' office and sat on the desk. She kicked off her shoe and used her stockinged foot to massage his groin. "I wish you had stayed on Friday."

"Not in here Tanya," Marcus said a little concerned.

Tanya smiled, "It's okay, nobody can see."

"It's too risky."

Tanya' s eyes lit up in excitement, "That's part of the fun!"

"Look if we're going to do this nobody can know."

"Well I'm not going to tell."

"I mean we've got to be really careful."

"I know."

"That means I can't see you till I've finished here.

"Why not?"

"I just think it's safer. Someone might twig. It's only till Wednesday," Marcus explained.

"They won't. I can be discreet."

Marcus smiled, "Well let's not take any chances."

"Whatever you say, but it'd better be worth the wait," Tanya relented, leaning forward to land a kiss.

"I'll meet you on Wednesday night - somewhere quiet."

"I know just the place," Tanya said.

"Will anybody…"

"Don't worry. I guarantee you no one will find out."

"Okay. I'll call you on your mobile and we'll meet in the street opposite the pub we went to."

"I thought you hadn't done this before?" Tanya said with a dirty smile broadened across her face.

"I haven't. I just can't afford to get caught."

Darren waited for the Prison Officer to give him his canteen sheet. Next week he would have all the required items, and his problems would be solved.

Claudia lifted the heavy duvet off her swollen belly and rose wearily from her bed. As she bent down to place her feet inside the slippers she moved her hands to her side in response to the kick she had just received from her unborn child.

Ken had swooned with delight the first time that he had felt her stomach and witnessed the baby kicking; but the novelty had worn off for Claudia. To be honest, the whole maternity thing was starting to lose its appeal.

With each day, she was gradually becoming more bored rigid; slowly turning into one of those people who woke at 10.00 a.m. but never got out of bed until the afternoon. There was nothing to look forward to in the day and her brain was bursting with frustration; screaming out, "I need to be used!"

She walked into the kitchen, made herself a cup of fruit tea and picked up the paper. She took in the lead story, which informed her that a British student had disappeared abroad. The picture of the girl and her black boyfriend triggered a switch in her mind. What was the name of the man in the Napier Court case again she pondered. She carried the cup through to the living room. Perhaps she might give Stephanie a ring. Maybe a review of the case might keep her occupied.

The Vectra drew neatly beside the pavement, and Marcus eased himself out and rose gracefully to his height. Dressed in a sleek two-piece suit with a tie that shone in the dark like his cheekbones, he portrayed the very essence of confidence.

Marcus unlocked the car and moved around its front to wait on the pavement. As he went his fingers rested a moment on the warm metal, a fond touch on the talisman that Natasha had bought him.

He glanced at a jewellers shop across the quiet road, then abruptly zapped the driver's door and coiled himself back inside, switched the ignition on and listened as a tape began to play. He shot a cuff and checked the time self-consciously.

It wasn't long before the quick tapping of cruelly high heeled, woman-in-a-hurry steps heralded a pretty, petite blonde in the headlights. She carried a shoulder bag clamped tight under her left arm. The black and white finger nails, black leather skirt and matching jacket over a low cut white top combined to make a tasteful impression of a woman dressed up with somewhere to go.

She was at a loss. Her eyes roving hungrily over the kerbs; small, keen ears pricked for the low throb of his car, both prey and predator embodied in the set of her narrow shoulders. When she saw the car she dived for it. With deliberation he released the passenger lock.

She caught her breath. "Sorry. I'm a bit late" she reached for him, kissed him. The parlour- painted nails in broad zebra stripes dug into his collar like little talons. She made a happy whimpering noise.

Sombrely Marcus set Tanya back, breaking the clinch.

"Where does your husband *think* you are?"

"Don't worry. I was careful. I'm very careful."

"Where does he think you are?" he repeated.

"Seeing a friend," Tanya said, beginning to sound sullen.

"Didn't he mind? Did he suspect anything?"

"Suspect what? As far as he's concerned I'm seeing a girlfriend. He's out with his mates watching a football match. He trusts me. He's not going to suspect anything. He's more concerned that his team win."

"So it's normal, you going out like this?

"What are you scared of? He didn't think anything."

"Nothing. Are you sure?"

Tanya made a big effort to be patient.

"Relax. I – was – very – very – careful."

Marcus came to some decision behind his eyes. "I'm sorry. I just worry that's all."

Tanya kissed him again and stroked his thigh. Marcus watched her hand with the black striped nails that were purple as death, black as orchids, white as platinum under the dirty sodium light. But although he liked the stroking and his back arched for it, he wasn't relaxed.

"But does your friend know what you're up to?" he wondered.

"For fuck's sake. There *is* no friend. He trusts me." And without irony she added, to settle it once and for all, "Why wouldn't he?"

Marcus persisted, as if he were a researcher administering a screening questionnaire.

"*Have* you cheated on him before?"

"Why do you call it cheating?" Tanya asked with a flounce and a twist, bringing her to stare at her own reflection in the passenger vanity mirror, which she adjusted.

These questions were turning her right off. Her husband wouldn't understand why she needed some attention and excitement. He'd been neglecting her needs for a while now since he had become confident of his ownership. So what if she found amusement elsewhere?

"Have you had any affairs then?" Marcus persisted.

"Yes twice. I love him, but things happen okay. As long as nobody gets hurt what harm is it doing?"

"He really doesn't have a clue?"

"No he doesn't. Look can we stop talking about him please."

Marcus leant across, stroked her blonde hair and planted a soft kiss on her lips, "fine by me."

He turned the key and the car purred gently to life. "Now where are we going?"

Tanya rummaged in her bag then produced a bunch of keys, which she jangled teasingly. "Perks of being in the property business," she smiled.

Marcus checked there was no traffic behind and smoothly eased the car on its way. "As long as nobody gets hurt," he whispered.

Darren finished writing the letter, sealed the envelope and addressed it. He hoped his mother would forgive him. He waited until the PO had made his late night check, then sat at the small table, smashed open the safety razor and removed the blades. Next,

185

he took the blue toothbrush and attached the blade with some string he had taken from a mop head to fashion a knife of sorts.

Darren examined his work, then satisfied with the result raised his weary body from the table, turned off the light and slumped across the small bed. The room was eerily quiet allowing all the noises from other prisoners to invade. Darren fluffed his solitary pillow; propped himself up and rolled up the sleeve of the prison issue shirt. With a tear in his eye, he took in a big lungful of air as he brought the blade to his exposed wrist.

Natasha waited until Candida had left with Guy before picking up the phone. After a tearful talk with Barbara at *The Old Spotted Mare*, she knew this call had to be made. If Alex had put doubts in Marcus' mind, he had to learn the truth from her. She chewed nervously on her fingernail as she dialled Marcus' mobile.

The drive was a short one, the city roads soon disappearing as the Vectra's headlights cut into the darkness. Marcus guided the car effortlessly through the country lanes while Tanya's hand gently stroked his thighs with promises of what was ahead.

He gripped the wheel tighter as he followed her instructions and turned into a quiet lane, which in turn led to a narrow private road. The car's headlights illuminated the 'For Sale' sign outside the secluded detached house.

"Perfect isn't it. No-one will disturb us" Tanya smiled as she leant across to kiss him. "I've been looking forward to this all week." She opened the door, swung her legs out, and waited for Marcus to join her. She took hold of his arm and they marched to the front door.

"Shit I forgot the champagne," Marcus apologized as she put the keys to the lock. "I'll just go back and get it."

He turned around, clicked on the zapper and opened the rear door, reached inside and picked up the bottle of champagne.

"Dirty cheap slag. Fucking whore," Marcus swore vehemently under his breath.

Marcus turned to leave, when his mobile phone rang. He fished in his pocket, brought out the phone and noted Natasha's familiar number.

Taff smiled as he read the text message that had just flashed on his mobile. He pressed the options button, selected call number and brought the phone to his ear.

"Hello, nice of you to call back."

A smile spread across the Welshman's face. "Well it's not everyday I get a message from a beautiful young lady telling me that they missed me."

"It's not everyday I say it. I really enjoyed last night. Shame you had to go to work this morning." There was a slight pause. "Any chance you might be interested in coming round again tonight?"

Taff imagined her face and knew instinctively she was enjoying teasing him. After last night it was obvious he would welcome the opportunity. The lovemaking had been gentle and comforting. Not what he had expected, but Melishia had certainly ticked all the right boxes.

"Might be worth your while," she said. "I'm making jerk chicken. And you can give me some more information about that Andrea Bailey woman you asked me about."

"What time will you be free?" he asked.

Stephanie Elford walked into her office and switched on the computer. She scrolled down and started reading the names on her database. She wrote the five names down on a piece of paper then wheeled the chair to the filing cabinet and pulled out the corresponding files.